SECOND SHOT

A MEN WITH WOOD NOVEL

C.M. SEABROOK

cm
SEABROOK

rynne

I HATE HIM.

The thought goes through my head the same second my traitorous body shivers in need from his touch.

"You shouldn't be here," Kane growls against my ear, his fingers tangling in my hair, his breath just as ragged as my own. His hard body is pressed to mine, trapping me against the wall in the entrance of his penthouse suite.

"Then let me go," I whimper, palms coming up to his chest in a pathetic attempt to push him away.

"Is that what you want?" The words tickle my cheek, sending another wave of warmth straight to my core.

What I want?

What I wanted was to come here and tell him off. To tell him he had no right talking about my brother the way he did during his post-game interview today.

He had no right to talk about Sam at all. No one does. Not when he's not here to defend himself.

Suicide. That's what the police report had called it a year ago today. What the media blasted across every news channel and newspaper. What Kane hinted at tonight in his interview.

It wasn't just his words, but his audacity to act like he fucking cared.

Kane Madden cares about no one but himself.

"I hate you." The bitter words come out in a choked sob and I see him wince slightly, but he doesn't let go, not even when I ball my fingers into fists and hit his chest. "I hate you."

"I know," he says through clenched teeth, resting his forehead against mine. "Hate me all you want if it makes you feel better."

His words twist inside me. "Don't do that."

"What?" He cups my face, his thumbs stroking across my jaw, intense blue eyes searching mine, making my insides melt and my knees go weak.

I hate that he can do that to me, even now, when I want nothing more than to blame him for everything.

"Don't act like you care."

He swallows hard and I see his nostrils flare, a touch of anger pulling at his lips. "Sam was my friend."

A vicious chuckle vibrates in my throat. "I'd hate to see how you treat your enemies."

Kane sighs and gives a harsh shake of his head. "I loved him like he was my fucking brother, Brynne. You know that."

I want to call bullshit, but I see my own pain mirrored in Kane's eyes, and something tugs inside my chest.

Hate. That's the emotion I need to hang on to. *Hate. Bitterness. Rage.* Because if I stop feeling those things, I know I'll be unable to resist the temptation in front of me.

I've heard people say that love and hate are two sides of the same coin. But with Kane, it isn't love; it's lust that distorts my feelings.

It doesn't matter how much I despise him, my body trembles anytime he's near. And right now, all six-foot-two inches of him is hovering over me like he's a predator and I'm his prey.

He's beautiful. Which I've always thought was a weird thing to call a man. But Kane is.

Being the daughter of Steve Jacobs, head coach of the Annihilators, I've been around hockey players all my life. But none look like Kane Madden.

It's not just his chiseled jaw, or the deep dimples in both of his cheeks when he gives one of his rare smiles. It's not even that the man's body is hard as granite, with muscles that ripple beneath naturally bronzed skin. It's his eyes. The lightest blue around the center, darkening to a deep cobalt around the edges.

Beautiful.

Everyone loves him.

Women.

Fans.

The media.

Especially my father.

I snort, and shake my head.

Kane is the son he always wanted. A son he could be proud of. And he'd made it known to Sam every chance he got. He never understood my brother, and he definitely never accepted him.

And now he's gone – *forever.*

"You think you're so perfect, don't you?" I cringe at the slight slur of my words, and when I speak again I try extra hard to pronounce each syllable carefully, but I'm pretty sure it just comes out forced. "You get everything you want. Don't you, *golden boy?*"

I curl my lips as I hiss the nickname my father gave him ten years ago when he was still playing in the juniors. A name that stuck even after he was drafted to the NHL.

Kane "The Golden Boy" Madden.

In the world's eyes, Kane Madden can do no wrong. But I know better. I know exactly who he is.

My worst enemy. The man who took my brother from me.

Kane's eyes narrow. "You've been drinking."

"So?" I jut my chin out at him defiantly. I don't usually drink, but tonight I finished an entire bottle of Chardonnay before calling an Uber to come here.

And it feels good.

It feels fucking terrific to finally let go.

"You're the last person who should be judging me."

"I'm not judging," he says past a frown, taking a small step back so he's no longer touching me.

I feel the loss of his heat immediately, and my body protests.

Kane rakes his hand through his thick, dark hair, and I have an urge to do the same, to feel those silky strands between my fingers as his face is buried between my thighs.

I lick my lips, and a small, silent moan builds in my chest.

"Brynne," Kane says sharply, his gaze hard.

"What?"

"Why are you here?"

Because I'm lonely. Because as much as I hate you, you're the closest thing I have left to Sam. Because I feel numb all the time, but when I'm around you I finally feel again, even if it's only anger. Because I can't stop thinking about your mouth, your hands, your body.

Because I need you.

A low growl rumbles from Kane's chest, and it's then that I realize I'd spoken the last four words out loud.

Shit.

"Brynne." My name is a deep, guttural rasp. He moves swiftly, capturing me against the wall, his hands firmly planted on either side of my head, his body barely touching mine, but I can feel the heat of his skin burning through the layers of clothes between us.

His gaze is intense and his breath feathers on my lips, smelling of scotch. I'm not the only one who's been drinking.

I can see the desire burning in his gaze. He wants to kiss me, and I'm dying for a taste of his lips. I've fought this – *him* – for so damn long.

"I hate you," I whisper, trying to hold on to my last ounce of strength.

"I know," he whispers back, just as his head lowers, his hand cradling the back of my head as his lips crash against mine.

I kiss him back.

Rough.

Hard.

Unapologetic.

"Brynne?" He says my name harshly, and I hear the question in his voice.

What are we doing?

I don't want to think. I just want to feel. To take. To use. To forget for one fucking minute how messed up this world really is.

"Don't say anything." Frantically, I tug at his shirt, needing to feel the warmth of his skin against mine.

He gives a small nod as if understanding, and reaches behind his head, pulling his shirt off and letting it fall to the floor.

Swiftly, his hands work my jeans down my hips, his

thumbs locking in my panties as he forces them down my thighs, while I struggle with his belt.

Our lips lash, and our tongues dance in a frenzy of desperate need. Years of pent-up longing boil over the surface, making everything seem *more* than it really is.

My fingers roam across his skin, across every line, every hard muscle, and I whimper, lost in him.

"Brynne." His touch slows, and I can hear the hint of concern in his voice.

I don't want his concern. I want his body. Nothing else.

"Don't stop," I beg, slipping my fingers into the waistline of his briefs and pushing them down until his heavy shaft springs free.

With a satisfied grunt, his hands are on my ass, and he lifts me up, so that my legs are wrapped around his waist and his cock rests hard against my entrance. He moves so that my back is against the wall, and he leans into me, holding me up with the weight of his body as his hands skate across my skin.

"Say it." His voice rumbles across the sensitive skin of my neck, where his lips rest. "Say you want this, Brynne."

"I want this," I moan, as he pulls back, so that the thick head of his cock nudges at my entrance.

No. I need this.

A cry of pleasure mixed with pain leaves me as he thrusts forward, filling me with one hard stroke.

I gasp, feeling pleasure within the deepest part of me.

I'm ready for him. Warm and wet. He pulls back, then slams into me again.

My muscles tighten around him, clenching with an urgency that builds quickly.

There's no tenderness in his movements. He takes me hard, fast, rough.

"Look at me, Brynne," he growls out, but I refuse.

Eyes clenched shut, fingers digging into his skin, I take what I need, and he uses me the same way.

One hand grips my hips as he continues to drive into me with deep, powerful strokes. His other hand reaches behind my head, tugging at my hair, and he demands, this time more forcefully, "Look at me."

I blink, my breath catching when I meet the blue of his gaze.

God, those eyes. Usually so hard and merciless, they hold a vulnerability now that makes my chest squeeze with emotions I have no right to feel.

Not able to hold his gaze any longer, I crush my lips against his, demanding the pleasure I can feel ready to explode through every nerve ending in my body.

Within seconds, my orgasm rips through me, a blinding ecstasy that sends flashes of white light behind my closed lids. Back arched, head tilted back, I cry out as wave after wave of pleasure rolls through me.

Kane isn't far behind. With one final thrust, he groans and spills himself inside of me so powerfully that I can feel the hot, heavy spurts at the back of my womb, causing my pussy to clench and spasm one more time around him.

His forehead rests against mine, and he breathes out roughly. "Jesus, Brynne."

We stay like that for a long moment, our sweaty bodies tangled as our breathing slowly returns to normal.

I don't want to move. I want to hold on to this feeling of euphoria that's already slipping away.

"Fuck," Kane mutters, still buried inside me, fingers tangled in my hair.

Guilt.

Regret.

I see it in his eyes when he pulls back to look at me.

"I shouldn't have done that."

I, not we. Like I was just some spectator in one of his depraved exploits.

Any connection I thought we had vanishes with those words.

"Don't worry, I'm not going to run to Daddy, if that's what you're worried about." Anger tightens my voice as I push him away.

He lets me, slowly lowering me to the ground and taking a small step backwards.

"That's not what I meant." There's a hollowness to his words that reminds me of the same empty void I carry around inside of me.

He pulls his pants up, tucking himself back in his briefs.

Keeping my gaze averted, I adjust my bra and shirt, then pull my jeans on, feeling the slickness of our pleasure cool and wet against my panties.

"We should talk." He rakes his fingers through his hair.

"There's nothing to talk about."

"Brynne. I care about you-" He reaches out to touch me, and I flinch, drawing back into myself, into the steel cage I've resurrected around my heart.

"Care?" I snort. "That's funny coming from you. Kane Madden doesn't care about anyone but himself."

Brick by brick, I reconstruct the wall around my heart.

He frowns and drops his hand, taking a step back, and has the nerve to look like I hurt his feelings.

Bullshit.

"What? Did you think that actually meant something to me?" I bold-faced lie. I chuckle darkly and shake my head. "You're nothing to me. And this—"I throw my hands up between us."—was just sex. Nothing more. That's the way you do it, right?" I narrow my eyes, going deeper into the abyss of resentment. "All those one-night stands you're so famous for. You know how this works better than me. Why try and complicate it with talking?"

His lips tug down further, and I see something cross his expression – *pain*. The kind of pain that breaks a person. Shatters them from the inside until they're completely numb.

Good. Let him feel it in every cell of his body.

I let the thought grow, let it fester, because I want him to hurt. I want to be the one to pierce through his cold, callous heart and make him feel the same brokenness that he's left me with.

When I turn to leave, I half expect, half hope he'll try and stop me.

He doesn't.

I shut the door behind me, my heart beating wildly in my throat, and the tears I've been holding back finally fall free across my cheeks.

I focus on why I came here tonight – *I hate Kane Madden.*

CHAPTER 1

One Year Later

ane

"YOU ALL RIGHT, OLD MAN?" Austin Branson chuckles as he unlaces his skates on the bench beside me. Dark blonde hair falls over his eyes before he does his signature head-flip thing that all the girls go ape-shit over.

The kid looks like he should be in a boy-band, not the starting forward for one of the best teams in the NHL.

I grunt and roll my shoulder, wincing when I hear the pop and crackle of my joints. I'm only eight years older than the kid, but today my body feels ancient and beaten down.

"You'd be feeling some pain, too, if you didn't have me protecting your ass out there." Today was only a practice, but even with our own guys, Coach has me watching the kid's back.

At twenty, he's the youngest starter on the team, and a

damn good player. But there's something wild, almost volatile underneath his cocky playfulness. He reminds me a little too much of myself at his age. Which means one thing – trouble.

Austin grins at me. "You coming to the Landing Strip tonight?"

"No." He's referring to the team's preferred strip club. The kid isn't even old enough to be in the damn place, but playing for the Annihilators has its perks. Free alcohol and easy women are just a couple.

"Guys are starting to spread rumors about you, bro. And I'm starting to wonder if they're not true. Haven't seen you with a chick since I joined the team."

"Fuck off, Branson." I toss my dirty towel at his face, and head to the showers.

Turning the water on, I step under the frigid stream, not adjusting the temperature, allowing the iciness to bite at my skin.

The kid is right. I've heard the guys talk. Wondering what my problem has been lately.

But it doesn't matter how many pairs of tits they try and push in my face, there's only one girl I can't stop thinking about – Brynne.

I fucked up, big time.

That night, a year ago, I knew she'd been drinking, and I knew how vulnerable she was. But I'd wanted her. Hell, I've always wanted her. For years I'd fought against the temptation to touch her, kiss her. Knowing I'd never have her. What it would mean to my career. My relationship with her family if I ever let myself have even a single taste.

I loved the woman more than was rational or sane. And she hated me in return.

Not that I hadn't given her reasons. I'd spent the past ten

years making sure those beautiful brown eyes never looked my way.

Brynne was in the kitchen the first time I saw her. Sitting at the table, legs curled up under her, light brown hair hanging over half her face, nose deep in a textbook and scribbling furiously on a notepad beside it.

"Dork, say hi to Kane," Sam flicked her ear as he passed, before opening the fridge and pulling out two bottles of beer, then handing me one. "He's going to be staying with us for a couple months."

Because I was still underage, Coach had made a deal with my foster parents to bring me into his house while I trained with the Annihilators' farm team. It was a good gig, and I wasn't about to screw it up.

Hockey was my life. The only thing that made me feel alive. Like I wasn't the fuck-up I'd always believed I was. On the ice, I was a god. And if the signing bonus the Annihilators were offering me was any indication of the money I'd be making, I was about to become one rich-ass mother fucker.

This house, and everything in it, could be mine one day. No more living off macaroni and cheese and ramen noodles. I was flying. Soaring to the top. And nothing was going to stop me.

"Hey," the girl mumbled, not looking up from her book.

"Don't mind her, she's anti-social. Aren't you, loser?" Sam teased.

Her head jerked up and she gave him a pointed glare. "Some of us actually want to graduate high school."

I felt something smack into my chest – *lust*.

She was prettier than I'd first thought. Soft, full lips, clear skin, free of make-up. She was a junior, I knew that from Sam. But there was something about the way she held herself that made her seem older.

"Who needs a high school diploma?" Sam placed his

13

empty bottle on the counter, and pulled out another one from the fridge. "Look at that Microsoft guy. He didn't graduate and he's like a multi-billionaire."

She rolled her eyes. "He dropped out of university, not high school. And trust me, you're no Bill Gates."

Sam chuckled and took a deep swig of his beer.

That's when her gaze finally rested on me. I'd been waiting for it. The draw. The flash of excitement when she finally saw me.

I was used to girls throwing themselves at me, used to the heated looks and shameless flirting. I'd leaned back against the counter, flexing my biceps as I brought the bottle to my lips, and gave her a cocky what-do-you-think look?

As expected, her gaze travelled down my torso, then back up to my face, and for a second I thought I saw a flicker of appreciation. But if it was there, it didn't last long.

Her lips pursed, and her eyes narrowed, before she'd dropped them back to the book she'd been studying from.

I should have left her alone, but I wasn't used to being dissed, and it was a blow to my ego.

"Whatcha reading?" I asked, turning a chair around and straddling it with my forearms resting on the back, and my bottle of beer dangling from my hand.

With a heavy sigh, she looked up at me. "Art history."

"You're an artist?"

"She's fucking incredible," Sam said, walking over to us and messing up her hair. "Aren't you, dork?"

The first hint of a smile tugged at her lips when she'd looked up at her brother, and it brightened her whole face.

I was wrong. The girl wasn't just pretty, she was fucking gorgeous.

She shrugged, cheeks infused with color.

"She's going to be the next Picasso, or what's that woman artist you're always going on about?"

"Frida Kahlo."

"Right. Your stuff is way better than hers," Sam said, unconcealed pride in his voice despite the way he teased her. "At least, it doesn't resemble a preschooler's art project."

Again, she'd rolled her eyes, but when she glared at him, there was affection in it, not like the cold judgement when her gaze took me in.

Even now, a decade later, I don't know why I was so desperate for her approval. *But I was.*

"You'll have to show me some of your work." Maybe I came on a little strong, leaning forward and giving her a dimpled grin that usually got me to second base with any chick, because the next thing I knew, she was pushing her chair back and slamming her textbook shut.

"I'll study in my room." She'd scurried from the room, but not before I'd gotten a good view of her perfect ass.

Sam slapped the back of my head and chuckled.

"What was that for?" I rubbed my neck, grinning, knowing full well why he'd hit me.

"Don't check out my sister, dude. So not cool."

I laughed, and made a promise I had no intention of keeping. "Won't happen again."

That she clearly hated my guts from the second she met me made things easier.

I kept my distance, or teased her mercilessly. Making sure she never looked at me like anything more than the trouble she clearly thought I was.

And she hadn't.

Or, at least, I thought she hadn't.

Not until she'd shown up at my apartment, eyes reflecting the same agonizing desire I'd been fighting all these years.

God, I wanted her.

But we were cursed from the start. And even if we hadn't been, I'd done enough to make sure she'd never fully trust me. Never see me for anything other than the bastard responsible for her brother's death.

"Madden." Blake Starowics, the Annihilators' first-string goalie and one of my closest friends, pops his head around the wall and slaps his hand on the tiles. "Coach wants to see you in his office."

Fuck.

I knew it was coming. The summons.

Teeth clenched, I turn the shower off and return to the change room, dressing slower than normal.

Most of the guys are gone.

Everyone but Blake and Sebastian.

I can feel their eyes on me, the tension radiating off them, the concerned glances they exchange.

"What?" I turn around, glaring between them.

They've been with the team as long as I have. Blake, one year more. And if I consider anyone my friend, it's these two. But right now, I know exactly what they're thinking, and the last thing I need is the fucking pity I see in their eyes.

"You okay?" Blake asks, leaning his elbows on his knees, his chin on his fisted hands.

"Shoulder's bugging me." I turn my back on them.

"Not what I meant."

Yeah, I know what he meant.

It's the two-year anniversary of Sam's death, and he's wondering if I'm going to self-implode.

Some days, I wonder the same thing.

You need to talk to someone, he'd said recently. *You're an emotional time-bomb.*

He's right. I am. Without the game to unleash my frustration and anger, I don't know how I would have gotten through the past couple of years.

I exhale heavily. "I'm fine."

"Bullshit," Sebastian mutters, leaning against the wall with his arms crossed. "You haven't been fine in a long time. You got to let it go, man. What happened with Sam wasn't-"

"Don't." I jerk my head around and pierce him with a warning glance. "Not today."

Sebastian sighs and places his hands up in a position of surrender. "All right. I'm just saying. No one blames you for what happened, except you."

And Brynne.

Because unlike everyone else, she knows the truth – I'm a fucking terrible friend.

Blake shakes his head as if reading my thoughts. "Come out with us tonight. Have a few drinks with the guys."

"Next time." I grab my bag and toss it over my shoulder.

I can hear their concerned mumblings as I leave the change room and head down the corridor towards Coach's office.

Pinching my eyes shut, I take a long, steadying breath before rapping my knuckles against his door.

"It's open." The words are hard, edged with a slur, and as soon as I open the door I see the opened bottle of whisky on his desk.

This won't be good.

Coach stands by the window, staring blankly out, swirling what's left of his drink in his right hand. Broad shoulders slouch forward, and when he turns I flinch at the haunted look in his eyes.

"You wanted to see me?" I force the words out, wishing I was anywhere but here.

He gives a hard nod, then moves back to his desk and pulls out a second glass, pouring the amber liquid into it before handing it to me.

I take a sip, silence stretching between us. Unsaid words filling the void.

Guilt isn't the only thing we share, but it's the one thing

that connects us more than anything else. Even more than hockey. Because as shitty of a friend as I was to Sam, Steve Jacobs was an even shittier father.

It's no wonder that Brynne hates us both.

After what seems like an eternity, he finally speaks. "Have you heard from Brynne?"

My gaze jerks up, but he's not looking at me. His eyes are glazed from the mixture of alcohol and whatever thoughts consume him.

For as long as I've known them, their relationship has always been volatile, strained, even before Sam died.

"No." I shake my head.

"I just thought...today..." His jaw twitches as he looks down into his glass. He shakes his head and stumbles to his chair, sitting down heavily. "I hoped she might have contacted you."

I'd hoped the same thing. Every fucking day for the past year.

He closes his eyes, leaning his head back. The man is only in his mid-fifties, but right now he looks at least ten years older. Silver threads through his once black hair, and deep lines that weren't there two years ago are etched into his face. But it's his eyes, sunken with dark circles, that really age him.

"You know what today is?" he slurs.

Of course I do.

"Yeah."

A strangling noise sounds in his throat, and I have to swallow back my own grief that threatens to choke me.

More silence.

His eyes remain closed, and long, strained minutes pass.

Eventually, his breathing becomes heavy and labored, and I'm pretty sure he's passed out.

Good.

Whatever gets him through this shitty day. I have similar plans of my own. A date with a bottle of scotch.

I place my glass on the desk and stand.

"Son." The word is slurred, but there's an agony, a desperation in that one word that slices through my heart. Because as much of an asshole the man was to his own kids, he's been like a father to me.

I wonder what he'd think of me if he ever found out what happened between Brynne and I?

There was always an unspoken rule.

She was off limits.

As cold and callous as he acted towards her, everyone but Brynne knew she was the fucking world to him.

"Yeah, Coach?"

His eyes open briefly. "If you hear from her, you'll let me know?"

I give a brisk nod, knowing I'm the last person she'd call.

CHAPTER 2

rynne

IN THE PASSENGER seat of Felix's new Mercedes Benz, I rub my palms across the rough fabric of my jeans and let out a slow, steadying breath as the car pulls to a stop in the cemetery parking lot.

My fist tightens around the flowers I brought. A bouquet of color conflicting with my mood, and the gray clouds that hang heavy above us.

Beside me, Felix turns the ignition off. He drags his hand through the dark, trimmed beard he's had since I met him at an art exhibit he'd hosted on campus during my freshman year. Over cheap Merlot and a heated debate about the differences between neo-impressionism and post-impressionism, we'd become quick friends. One of the few friends I'd kept in contact with the past couple of years.

"You okay?" he asks.

"Yeah," I lie, hating how pathetic my voice sounds.

I'm tired. And not just physically. Emotionally. Mentally. I'm exhausted, my secret a burden that's become almost too difficult to bear.

Glancing over my shoulder, a small, sad smile tugs at my lips when I catch the profile of my son's face. He's still so tiny. Little fingers curl into tight fists, and his bow-like lips pucker in a sucking motion in his sleep.

He looks like Kane. My chest squeezes like it always does when I see the resemblance, because it's a reminder that I can't keep him to myself. One day soon, I need to stop being a coward and tell him.

I've tried. Several times. But fear had paralyzed me.

Fear of facing him again.

Fear that he'd want to be part of Noah's life.

Fear that he wouldn't.

Fear that, like Sam, I'd lose Noah, too.

"You sure you're all right?" Felix asks, placing his large hand over mine, dark eyes filled with concern.

Felix is good looking in that clean-cut, GQ-like way, but he's never been more than a friend. And right now, that's all I need. All I have time for. Not to mention that the small part of my heart that I actually let feel something was consumed years ago by a boy who could never love me back. A boy who would taint and destroy the only person who ever really cared about me.

"I'm fine." I give his fingers a small squeeze, then pull away, breaking the intimacy he's created. "Thanks for driving."

"Anytime. Anything you and Noah need, I'm here for you."

He's proven it. Driving me to doctors' appointments, lending me money when I was late on rent, even getting me an exhibition night at Gwen Siders' next month.

That's if I can finish something that doesn't make people

flinch and recoil into themselves when they see it.

It isn't that my paintings are bad. Technically, they're flawless. But even I know that they're lacking something.

Mechanical and cold, one reviewer had said. *Holding nothing of the artist's essence.*

I'd laughed bitterly at that, because they were wrong. It wasn't that my heart and soul weren't poured out on the canvas - it's that they were.

Mechanical.

Cold.

Two words that describe me perfectly.

I'd turned off my emotions years ago. The only thing that had made me feel was Kane.

And now Noah.

I could run from Kane. But not from the child we'd created. And the emotions he stirred inside me were, at times, scary as hell.

Because I loved him.

And one thing I've learned in life is that the things you love are always taken from you.

"You want me to come with you?" Felix asks, when I don't get out of the car.

"No. I need to do this alone."

He nods, then places his hand behind the seat, stretching out as he glances backwards at Noah. "We'll just hang out here."

I try to return his smile, but my face feels strained, and even the motion of opening the car door takes every ounce of my strength.

It rained earlier, and the grass is still damp, squelching under my feet as I make my way through the maze of headstones.

It's been a year since I've been here. *Too long.*

I swallow past the lump in my throat when I find the two

headstones that have JACOBS printed across the top.

AUDREY JACOBS.
   Beloved wife and mother.

"HI, MOM." I place my hand on the cool stone as I crouch down and place the flowers I brought in the metal stand. There's a small engraved picture of her above her name that's been smoothed out from the elements. I trace my fingers over the soft lines of her face. A face that looks so much like mine. It's odd to think that she wasn't much older than I am now when she died.

I never felt any deep sadness when my father used to bring us as kids. Maybe it was because I was too young to remember her. Too young to really feel her loss. But with Sam, I feel his loss in the very center of my being, like a hot knife stabbing my chest every time I think about all the things he'll never experience.

Like meeting his nephew for the first time.

I inhale shakily and stand, tears pricking at the back of my eyes as I read my brother's name, and the pathetic epitaph my father picked out.

ADORED SON.
   Forever remembered.

THE BITE of bitterness sinks into me, warring with the suffocating pain of loss.

"I'm sorry I haven't been here in a while," I whisper, wrapping my arms around my chest and shivering as a cool breeze blows around me. "I did that art exchange we always talked about. It was supposed to be six months in Rome and six in France, but..." I swallow hard and blink back tears. "I only made it to Rome."

I was there five months when I realized I was pregnant. It was Felix that mentioned it when he'd come to visit. He'd made a joke that I'd either been enjoying the pasta and pizza a little too much, or I was pregnant.

I'd laughed about it, until I'd tried to remember the last time I'd had my period.

"I can't be." I'd denied it fiercely, even as the truth blared like a siren in my head. "I've had sex once in the last year, there's no way..."

Felix held the positive pregnancy test, brows raised. "Looks like once was enough."

It was just my luck. Like the universe was laughing at me. Or punishing me for that one night.

"I had a baby, Sam." It's weird to say it out loud, even if it's only to the wind. "He's beautiful." *So damn beautiful.* "He's completely bald, but his eyelashes are light, almost translucent. I think he's going to be blonde like...you."

I'm rambling, talking like Sam can hear me, even though I know he can't. But I need this. The connection. Even if it's just in my head.

"He started smiling last week, and when he does, he has dimples in both cheeks. He looks so much like..." I whisper the next two words. "...like Kane."

A crow squawks above me as if in protest to my admission.

"It shouldn't have happened. I never meant..." I squeeze my eyes shut. "I hate him for what he did to you. For what he made you become. For taking you from me. But I hate myself even more for betraying you."

Because that's what that night was. A betrayal. After

everything Kane did, what he didn't do. I should never have talked to him again, let alone let him touch me. Kiss me. Consume me.

And he did. I'd held my heart back for years. Or, at least, I thought I had. But with one taste of his lips, every frozen, broken piece of my soul had sparked. And I'd felt something. Something I had no right feeling. Something that I knew would destroy me if I'd stayed.

"I haven't told him," I whisper the confession.

The crow squawks again, louder this time, perching on one of the nearby headstones, watching me with beady black eyes, head twisting from side to side.

"Felix has been helping me." I inhale through my nose, then let out a slow, uneven breath. "He's been a good friend. Helped me find an apartment, and set up a corner for a studio, so I can still paint when Noah is sleeping. Which isn't often. But I've started to sell some of my paintings…"

God, now I'm lying to a ghost.

I pinch my eyes shut, tilting my head to the sky, letting the first few drops of rain mingle with my tears.

"I miss you so much, Sam." My throat burns. "I wish you were here. I know you'd want to kick my ass if you were. But…" I crouch and place my palm on the stone over Sam's name and close my eyes. "If you can hear me, give me a sign. Tell me what the hell I'm supposed to do."

The crow squawks one last time before flying off. The flap of wings and the whistling of the wind is the only response.

"Brynne?" My name is a shocked slur behind me, followed by the squish of footsteps on wet grass.

My chest tightens.

I don't need to turn to know who the voice belongs to. Deep and scratchy, that one word burns like fire through my body, while at the same time sending a chill down my spine.

Kane.

Shit. Shit. Shit.

Not today. I can't do this. Not now.

Slowly, painfully, I stand and turn, inhaling sharply at the man who stands in front of me.

Dark scruff shadows the angles of his jaw, and his hair sticks up in different directions like he's run his fingers through it in frustration. But it's his eyes, a piercing blue rimmed with red, that has my chest squeezing.

Kane Madden is not a small man, but as he takes a step towards me, he looks – *broken.*

Emotions coil and curl inside me.

Anger.

Desire.

Bitterness.

Longing.

It doesn't seem possible to feel so many contrary emotions for one person.

He stands there, watching me with what looks like affection and relief, and a stupid thought pops into my head. *Maybe everything will be okay. Maybe he's not the demon I've made him out to be. Maybe we can make things work.*

Reckless thoughts.

But I allow them a moment of freedom.

That is, until my gaze drops to the half-empty bottle of scotch in his hand.

He's drunk. Defiling Sam's grave just with his presence.

Damn him.

He takes a step towards me, staggering. "Jesus, Brynne. It's good to see you."

I snort out a vicious laugh, because some things never change, and Kane Madden is one of them. "I wish I could say the same."

 ane

AFTER COACH'S OFFICE, I'd left the arena and walked. I had no idea where I was going, other than a liquor store. Vison hazy, brain dimmed by alcohol and grief, I'd let my feet guide me. It wasn't until I was threading my way through trees and headstones that I knew where I was.

The fucking cemetery. Walking through the stone labyrinth, I'd slammed back half a bottle of scotch, trying to find Sam's gravestone.

I'd been ready to give up, when I saw her.

Brynne.

Crouched over Sam's grave, her guard down, I saw the vulnerability that she always tried so hard to hide from the world. And in that moment, it took every last ounce of self-preservation not to scoop her up, wrap my arms around her, and not let go.

She hates you, jackass, my brain warned. *She doesn't want you here. She doesn't want you anywhere near her.*

When her gaze met mine, her emotions unguarded for a split second, I swear I saw straight into her soul. And in it, the reflected loss, the need to connect, the longing for more.

But just as quickly, her expression changed when her gaze landed on the bottle in my hand.

Eyes hardened, and the connection I'd felt seconds before was gone.

The way she looks at me now, disgust turning up her lips, makes my stomach twist.

"Brynne." Her name on my lips is a tortured cry, and I hate myself for how fucking pathetic I must seem to her.

With a sharp shake of her head, she turns on her heels and moves quickly through the gravestones towards the parking lot.

"Brynne, stop." I toss the bottle away and catch up to her in three long strides, seizing her forearm and pulling her towards me.

"Let me go." I feel the tremble that races through her small body, and greedily I take it, take anything other than the hate I see in her eyes.

"We need to talk." My words are slurred; even I can hear it.

"You're right, we do. But not like this. Not here. Not when you're drunk…" Her gaze hardens. "Or high."

I drop her arm and drag my fingers over my face roughly. "I don't do that shit. Never fucking have."

She makes a sound at the back of her throat, one filled with disbelief and contempt. And I know in that second that even if I told her the full truth, she'd never believe me.

"You shouldn't be here, Kane."

"He was my friend. Whatever you believe about me, you can't deny that."

She opens her mouth to protest, but I stop her.

"I know you blame me for what happened. I get it."
Emotions I haven't let myself feel burn in my chest and
squeeze my throat, making it difficult to breath. "But I'm
hurting, same as you."

Silence.

I expect her to turn and walk away, or yell at me. What I
don't expect is the small amount of sympathy I see in
her eyes.

"I know." The words are still full of the anger she tries so
desperately to hold on to. But there's something else. A tired-
ness. Like she doesn't have the strength to argue with me.

And that worries me more than the constant battle she
fights against me. Because the one thing Brynne isn't,
is weak.

Part of me wonders if I should have told her the truth
straight from the start. Maybe it would have shifted some of
the blame away from me. She wouldn't hate me as much as
she does. But I swore to Sam I'd protect her. And the only
way I know how to do that is keeping her brother up on the
fucking pedestal where she placed him.

A tear slides down her cheek, and I reach out, catching it
with the back of my hand, grazing my knuckles across the
soft skin. Her eyes close, and she lets out a small sound that's
a mix between a whimper and a sob.

I hate that she's hurting. Hate that I'm partially responsible for it. And I fucking hate that I can't do anything to
fix it.

We stand there in silence. My hand resting on her cheek.
Her eyes closed. Our bodies close. The cold wind that whips
around us is a stark contrast to the heat that burns
between us.

Her lashes flutter open, gaze holding mine, and I get a
glimpse of what we could have. Walls down. Heart exposed. I
see her. Every beautiful, broken piece.

"I haven't been able to think about anything but you."

"Kane, don't-"

"Your touch." I trace her mouth with the pad of my thumb, and she whimpers. "Your lips. The way your body fit perfectly against mine."

Even though I realize that if I let anything happen between us again, it'll probably destroy us both, I can't stop myself from slipping my other hand behind her neck, cupping the back of her head and leaning down so that our lips are only a breath apart.

She releases a shuddering breath and closes her eyes. "Kane...please...don't do this."

"I haven't stopped thinking about you. Wanting you."

Walk away, asshole.

"Don't," she whimpers again.

"That night. I should have taken my time. Should have... protected you."

She shakes her head, but doesn't move away. "It was wrong."

"Maybe, but it felt right. You can't deny that."

"Kane. I-"

I'm about to press my mouth against hers, show her how right it feels, when a baby's cry echoes behind us, followed by a man's deep voice. "Everything okay here?"

Brynne's face drains of color before she pulls away from me, taking a stumbling step backwards.

She glances over at the guy and stutters, "Fine. Everything's fine."

"Sorry." The man shifts the baby in his arms, but it continues to squawk. "I couldn't get him to settle down."

A coldness settles in my chest. Who the hell is this guy and why is he staring at Brynne like he expects her to take the kid from him?

Brynne looks between him and me, fear flashing in her

eyes, before her shoulders drop in resignation, and she walks towards the asshole who's staring daggers at me now.

When she takes the baby from his arms, it stops crying immediately.

My stomach twists, all sorts of scenarios racing through my head. And despite finishing off three-quarters of a bottle of scotch, I suddenly feel stone-cold sober.

She places her hand on the guy's arm, and I feel the touch like a blow to the gut.

With deep olive skin and dark eyes with slicked back hair like one of those douchebags on the cover of a fucking magazine, the guy is too good looking for his own good. Gray slacks and alligator-skin shoes. White button-down shirt with sleeves rolled to the elbow and the first few buttons undone, exposing dark chest hair. He's got the whole pretty-boy look that makes me want to punch him in his perfect, bleached teeth.

I hate him immediately. Especially when he looks at Brynne with a possessiveness that only I have the right to, making the caveman inside of me stand up and bang his fists against his chest.

Brynne says something to him in a hushed tone that has him turning his gaze back on me. His jaw begins to tick, and his eyes roam up and down my body, sizing me up.

That's right, fucker. Take a good look. He's tall, but I'm taller, and outweigh him by a good thirty pounds of muscle.

Brynne says something else that has his nostrils flaring, but he gives a small nod, placing his hand on her shoulder, before turning and heading back towards the parking lot.

A million questions itch on my tongue, but I keep my mouth clamped shut, and I realize that it's fear of knowing the truth that stops me.

She adjusts the baby on her shoulder. I can't see its face,

only the dark blue jumper with the hood covering the kid's head.

Blue. Which I assume means it's a boy.

Rubbing the back of my neck, I finally ask, "He's yours?"

She tugs her bottom lip between her teeth and gives a small nod.

Fuck.

More silence. She keeps looking at me like she's expecting some type of reaction.

I don't know what I'm supposed to be feeling, but I know what I shouldn't be – jealousy. What started out as a small flicker when I saw her touch the guy has become a burning inferno.

"You two married?" I nod towards the parking lot, where I can see the guy watching us from the driver's seat of a Mercedes Benz.

Pompous ass.

"Who?" She glances over her shoulder, following my gaze. "Me and Felix?" When she looks back at me. her brows are drawn down like she's the one confused. "He's just a friend."

I want to call bullshit. Friends don't look at friends the way he'd been looking at her.

"He's not the..." I swallow hard, struggling with the word. "Father?"

"No." She shifts the baby in her arms and I get the first glimpse of him.

Blue eyes blink up at her, and a small smile exposes deep dimples in both cheeks.

I take a step closer, my breathing speeding up. "How old is he?"

Brynne hesitates before answering. "Three months."

I can practically feel the adrenaline releasing into my blood as I do the calculation in my head.

There's no fucking way the kid is mine. Even as I think it, I know the truth.

"Kane, I..." She looks terrified. "I'm sorry. I...was going to tell you-"

"Tell me?" The words come out louder and with more anger than I intended, and I see her flinch. Grinding my back teeth, I breathe in through my nose and try to gather some semblance of patience. But I'm holding onto threads. Because I'm more than angry. I'm fucking pissed. "All right. Then tell me."

She opens and closes her mouth, tears gathering in her eyes. But I'm all out of compassion. I just want to know the truth. To hear it from her lips.

"I..."

"Brynne." Her name is a low growl that comes from somewhere deep in my throat. "Is. He. Mine?"

Her only response is a small nod. It's enough. I have my answer.

"Jesus Christ, Brynne." I drag both hands through my hair. *I have a kid.* But as much as a mentalfuck as that is, what's even more disturbing is that she kept it from me. "You weren't going to tell me?"

"I was. I just..."

It's a lie. I can hear the truth in her voice. She's always been a shitty liar.

I cup the back of my head, pulling at my hair, needing something to do with my hands so I don't throttle her.

"Does your dad know?"

"No."

Fuck. When Coach finds out, he's going to have a goddamn aneurysm. Then he's going to kill me. Or her. Maybe both of us.

"God, Brynne. What were you thinking?"

"Don't put all the blame on me."

33

"That's not what I meant. You had my kid and you didn't tell me. I don't care how much you hate me. That's pretty messed up."

My anger seems to have sparked her own. I can see it in her eyes even before she opens her mouth to speak.

"Maybe I should have told you-"

"There's no maybe. He's my kid. I deserved to know."

The baby lets out a rattling cry.

Brynne rocks him, and I can see the tears gathering in her eyes. "Stop yelling."

"I'm not yelling," I say loudly, before taking a deep breath, and lowering my voice. "But I have every right to."

"Why? Because you want this? You want to be a father? God, Kane, look at your life." She juts her chin out, still glaring at me despite the tears that now stream freely down her cheeks. "You know we're better off without you."

Her words are worse than any physical blow. I've taken a lot of shit from her over the years, but this tops it all.

"I'm so fucking tired of being the villain in your head. I'm not the monster you think I am, Brynne."

She presses her lips to the baby's forehead and clenches her eyes shut. I know what she's doing, what she's always done around me. She's closing her eyes to who I am so that she doesn't have to see the truth.

The baby keeps crying, and something in my chest tightens. I want to hold him. To protect him. To be the father he deserves.

And I will be. Whether she likes it or not.

"He's my son, Brynne. I *will* be in his life." It's not just a promise, it's a demand.

Her eyes open, and for a long tense moment she holds my gaze as if searching for something. Whatever it is, I don't think she finds it, because she shakes her head.

"He's hungry. I have to go." She starts to turn.

"Wait," I growl out, before she has the chance to dart away. I don't want to let her – *them* – go, because I'm afraid if I do, I'll never see them again. "You didn't tell me his name."

"Noah." She exhales shakily before adding, "Noah Samuel."

My chest squeezes. "It's a good name."

She nods, glancing over at the car where her *friend* is still glaring at me with as much jealousy as I feel.

"Where are you living?"

"I'll text you-"

"Brynne."

She hesitates before answering. "Inverness and Pine."

I frown because I know exactly what type of housing is there, and there's no way in hell I'm going to allow her to raise my kid in that neighborhood. But I'm sober enough to know that this isn't the time to argue about it.

When she turns to walk away again, I let her.

I watch until the car pulls away, down the long road, disappearing behind the stone wall.

My knees buckle and I sit down heavily on the wet grass, leaning against one of the cold stones, my new reality pressing down on my shoulders like a heavy boulder.

I'm a father.

It changes everything.

Brynne was right when she'd said I hadn't wanted it. I'd never thought about being a parent. I'm a selfish son-of-a bitch. And the world I live in isn't exactly family-oriented. Coach was proof of that.

I've got a son. Maybe the thought should be more terrifying than it is. But it's not.

If anything, it just gives me a reason to finally take what I've wanted for too damn long.

CHAPTER 4

Seven Years Ago

rynne

"I CAN'T BELIEVE Kane Madden is in your basement," Amber squeals, glancing in the mirror above my dresser and running her fingers through her platinum blonde hair.

I roll my eyes and flop down on my bed with the art history book I'm supposed to be reviewing for my exam on Monday.

"He's just a hockey player." I've been around them all my life, and Kane Madden is no different. At least, that's what I keep telling myself, hoping one day my stupid heart will realize the truth.

"You mean a hockey god." She giggles like she's a freshman in high school rather than college. "He's gorgeous."

"He's okay," I shrug, ignoring the butterflies that never fail to take flight whenever Kane's name is mentioned. I hate that he has that effect on me. The ability to make my fingers tingle and my heart race. But no matter how hard I try to focus on the cocky arrogance he reeks of, my knees go weak every time he turns that dimpled smile on me.

"Come on, you have to introduce me," she whines, jumping on the bed, and pulling my textbook out of my hands and tossing it across the bed. She folds her hands in front of her face and bats her eyelashes at me, begging, "Please."

I exhale heavily. "Fine. But we're not hanging out with-"

"Thank you. Thank you. Thank you." She wraps her arms around me in a tight hug. "You're my freaking hero, you know that?"

I roll off the bed and shake my head at her enthusiasm. I get that not everyone grew up with Steve Jacobs as their father, and an endless stream of professional hockey players coming in and out of their house on a regular basis, but being the daughter of the Annihilators' coach isn't as glamourous as Amber and her sorority friends seem to think it is.

"Is that your brother?" Amber asks, bending over to look at the framed picture on my dresser of Sam and I at my high school graduation.

Sam's got his arm slung around my shoulder, his sandy brown hair hanging carelessly over his forehead, and an I-don't-give-a-fuck-about-life smile plastered across his face.

That's Sam. Carefree. Fun. Gliding through life without a worry for tomorrow. The opposite of everything I am. It's what I love about him, but it's also what keeps getting him into trouble.

"Is he a hockey player, too?" Amber asks, licking her lips like he's an appetizer, with every intention of taking a bite.

"No. Not anymore." He stopped playing a couple of years ago. Knee injury. But I know he was secretly relieved. He'd always hated the pressure our dad put on him.

I'm no Kane Madden, Sam always said, whenever anyone asked him if he played. He said it with a casual smile. But we both knew it was a way to hide the hurt that our father loved the man more than his own kids.

"Too bad. He's cute," Amber says, still giggling.

I give an annoyed grunt, hearing her hidden meaning. He wasn't worth her time.

"Do I look okay?" Amber asks, pulling her t-shirt lower to expose more cleavage. Even for a study session, she looks like she's ready to go clubbing. And I'm starting to wonder if her recent insistence that we study here rather than the university library or her dorm wasn't for some ulterior motive. That motive being Kane Madden.

It's no secret that my brother and Kane are friends, or that they like to party together. There are pictures all over social media to prove it. Sam worships the ground Kane walks on, just like my father.

I get my father's obsession. Kane is talented. Probably one of the best defenders in the league. But he's arrogant. Cocky. And I have every intention of being the one Jacobs not to fall for his charms.

But secretly I already know it's too late for that.

A quick peek in the mirror, and I groan inwardly. With my hair tied on top of my head in a messy bun, and over-sized, dark-framed glasses that keep falling down my nose, I don't need to worry about catching Kane's attention. At least, not any positive attention.

Amber is more his type; blonde, busty, with a sexual confidence that I could never pull off.

"Well?" Eyebrows raised, she waits for my answer.

Ignoring the pinch of jealousy that makes my back teeth clench, I answer, "You look beautiful."

"I know, right?" She laughs, blue eyes a little too bright,

and I have a feeling that if given a chance, she won't be leaving here alone tonight.

Not that I care. She can do whatever she wants, with whoever she wants.

Just not with Kane, my stupid heart protests.

"Come on," I mutter, leading her downstairs to the large rec room in the basement.

The TV is blasting a baseball game and music blares from a stereo. Kane and Sam are spread out on the oversized leather couches. They don't see us. I'm about to shout out for them to turn down the volume, until I see what Sam's doing.

With a rolled dollar bill in his hand, he leans over the coffee table and snorts one of the four lines of white powder in front of him.

"Oh my God," Amber whispers behind me. "Is that…"

Cocaine.

I've never seen the stuff, other than in movies, but there's no denying what it is.

Sam closes his eyes, inhaling deeply through his nostril, then hissing out a breath. When he opens his eyes, they're glossy, his pupils so big they look like empty black holes.

"That's good stuff, bro," Sam says, reaching out to hand Kane the rolled bill.

Kane leans forward as if to take it from him, but when he does, he must catch my reflection in the TV, because his head jerks around.

"Shit," Kane hisses.

Sam glances over at me, and he smiles. *He fucking smiles.* "Hey, dork. Who's your friend?"

I'm pretty sure my brain has stopped working because I can't move, can't think. All I see are the drugs spread out in front of him like a narcotic smorgasbord.

"What the effing hell, Sam."

"What?" He leans back on the couch, his gaze roaming down Amber's body, and a lazy grin stretching his face.

"You're kidding me, right?" Words finally spill from my lips. "You're doing drugs now?"

And not just any drug; the mother of all drugs. Sam's always been a partier, but I'd never have thought he'd touch the stuff. Shit, he's still a month away from being able to go to the bars legally.

"Relax, dork. It's Friday night," Sam says, patting the couch for Amber to join him.

And she freaking does.

"We're just having a little fun. Not hurting anyone." Sam picks up a beer bottle from the table, lifting it to his lips, as he drapes his arm over Amber's shoulder.

Disappointment and anger mixes with my initial shock.

Sam has been acting odd the past few months. Staying out for days at a time. Sleeping when he is home. More irritable than normal. I thought it was just the pressure my dad put on him to get a job. Be a responsible adult. But now I'm wondering if it isn't something more.

Kane's gaze hasn't left me. His dark hair, which usually falls in dark waves across his forehead, is pushed off his face, and his brows knit together as he takes me in, his expression severe. I can't read his thoughts, but what I want to see is guilt. Because there's no way this shit was my brother's idea.

"You're both idiots, you know that?"

Kane winces, but Sam's attention is zeroed in on the ballgame.

"Amber, let's go."

Wrapping her skinny body around Sam, she meets my gaze with a look of triumph. "Your brother's right. It's Friday night. Come on, Brynne, loosen up."

Loosen up? Is she serious?

Sam snickers, glancing back at me. "Yeah, loosen up, dork."

I love my brother. More than anyone in this shitty world. But I hate what he's become since he started hanging out with the man who's watching me with stormy eyes filled with guilt.

I shake my head, spinning on my heels, and I storm back up the stairs.

"Brynne," Kane's deep voice growls out behind me.

"Get lost, Madden."

"Damn it, Brynne. Wait." He grabs my arm, spinning me around, so that I'm practically nose to nose with him.

I should look away, not tempt the predator lurking behind the blue eyes that stare down at me. Instead, I jut my chin out at him defiantly.

"What?" I do my best to ignore the heat of his touch, but it's nearly impossible. It sizzles through me. Hot. Demanding. Tempting.

"Let me explain."

"Explain? Explain what?" I glare at him, pouring all my disappointment, all my fear for Sam into the look. "I always knew you were bad news. I just didn't know how bad."

His nostrils flare and he holds my gaze, something warring behind his eyes. He releases me, then drags his hands over his face.

"My dad is going to flip when he finds out."

He lets out a slow breath. "Are you going to tell him?"

The way he asks, I wonder if he wants me to.

I should. But I know what he'd do. His *golden boy*, Kane, might get a slap on the wrist. But it would be worse for Sam. My father's wrath is always worse for my brother. If he thought for even a second Sam was doing drugs, he'd kick him out of the house. He already threatened to when Sam dropped out of university last year.

"No." I push on his chest, which considering I'm almost a foot shorter and he outweighs me by a hundred pounds, is pretty pointless.

He doesn't budge. Just looms over me, all brooding and intense.

"You want to screw up your own life, fine. But don't drag my brother down with you."

"You always want to think the worst of me." He leans closer, his blue gaze searching mine with an intensity that makes me shiver. "Why is that?"

Because you scare me. Because I don't trust my heart around you. Because you make me feel the one thing I'm terrified of being – weak.

"Maybe it's because I just found you snorting cocaine in my basement. Hard to talk your way out of that one, Madden."

"I didn't…" His jaw muscles bounce as he glances over his shoulder.

"Didn't what?"

He doesn't answer, just stands there glaring down at me. I know I should walk away, but all I can do is focus on the dark stubble on his jaw, the way he pulls his full bottom lip between his teeth, and the way he runs his fingers through his hair causing his biceps to flex and strain the fabric of his t-shirt.

His eyes glide down my body from head to toe, then back up, halting on my lips.

Electricity.

Lust.

Attraction.

All those things and more burn in his gaze. He shoves his hands in the pockets of his designer jeans, his lips tightening into a thin line, the blue of his gaze so intense I can't help but shiver.

Danger rolls off him, but I don't know how to stop my body from responding to his.

A wall of anger. That's the best way to guard my heart. Brick by brick, I lay the foundation. I may not be able to keep my brother from trouble, but I can protect myself.

"If anything happens to him, I'll blame *you*."

The muscles in Kane's jaw tense, and he says before he walks away, "Trust me, Brynne. I know."

CHAPTER 5

Present

 ane

THE RINK HAS ALWAYS BEEN the place where I could clear my head. Game. Practice. Doesn't matter. Just putting the gear on, the sound of metal against ice, the smell of leather and sweat, the feel of the stick in my hands; it's an adrenaline rush. A place to channel my aggression. And today, I have a lot of fucking aggression.

Coach has us working on a two-v-two drill that has me and Austin pitted against Sebastian and one of the newest additions to the team, Tyler Slade. Usually, I can outskate both of them, but today my feet feel like they have concrete blocks rather than skates attached to them.

Tyler gives me a little bump from behind, before maneuvering around me and taking the puck away. Using all of my

44

two-hundred-and-twenty pounds, I check him into the boards, and he drops - hard.

"What the hell?" Tyler is up quickly, gloves fisted in my jersey.

I push him back. "Lay off, asshole. It was a clean shot."

The man mumbles something under his breath and drops his hands. I should let it go. Usually, I would. But I'm itching for a fight.

When he starts to turn, I give him a swift uppercut to the jaw, not hard enough to do any real injury, but enough to cause a reaction.

And I get one.

His gloves come off and his fist connects with my face, a blow that's going to do some damage. But it feels good. It feels fucking great.

My own gloves come off, and I get a few good shots in of my own, before the guys are pulling me off him.

Blake and Sebastian hold me back, Coach is screaming, and Tyler is bleeding all over the damn ice. But the only thing I can think about is Brynne - and the kid.

"Get off me." I shrug away from Blake and Sebastian.

"Madden," Coach has fire in his eyes, and it's aimed straight at me. "Get over here."

I can't deal with him. Not right now. My head is a mess. And every time I look at the man, I can't help but play his words from the other night over and over in my head.

If you hear from her, you'll let me know.

Jesus, what am I supposed to tell him? *Yeah, I not only saw her, but also the grandkid she hasn't told you about. Oh, and by the way, I'm the fucking father.*

Ignoring Coach's hollering, I skate off the ice.

I didn't sleep last night. And I know I won't until I see her again.

The initial shock has worn off, at least slightly, enough to

45

know that I'm more than pissed at her. Fuck her reasons. The kid is as much mine as it is hers, and I'll be damned if I'm going to let her keep him from me.

The fact that she thought for even a second that I wouldn't want to be part of his life only frustrates me more. Sure, the thought of having a kid never really crossed my mind. But I'll be damned if I'm going to let my own son grow up the same way I did, not knowing who his father is.

In the change room, I tear my helmet off and toss it on the bench, before slamming my fist into the wall.

"Jesus, Madden." Blake moves into the room, pulling off his goalie mask and dragging his fingers through his long, dark hair. Gray eyes watch me carefully, like he's ready at any second for me to detonate. "What's going on with you?"

"Nothing." I sit down and start unlacing my skates.

Still in his heavy gear, he sits down on the bench across from me. "You going to tell me or am I going to have to beat it out of you?"

With my elbows on my knees, I place my head in my palms and mutter, "Brynne's back."

Silence.

I look up, expecting some response, but he's just watching me with a you're-asking-for-trouble look.

"Does Coach know?"

I shake my head. "I was at the cemetery yesterday. She was there…"

"You going to tell him you saw her?"

"I don't know." I scrub my fingers over my face. "I don't know what the hell I'm going to do."

More silence.

"You want to tell me what's really going on?"

I exhale heavily, then mutter, "She's got a kid."

He frowns. "And that's your problem, how?"

I hold his gaze, jaw clenched, waiting. I can see the

moment he gets it. His eyes widen and his mouth drops open.

"Fuck. It's yours? Jesus, Kane. You slept with her?" With every word, his voice gets louder.

"Keep your voice down."

"Coach is going to have your balls when he finds out."

"Right now, Coach is the least of my worries." Pinching the back of my neck, I look up at the ceiling, then close my eyes. "She doesn't want me having anything to do with him." I huff out a bitter laugh. "I don't think she'd even have told me if I hadn't seen him."

Blake exhales loudly. "That's messed up, man."

"Yeah."

"What are you going to do?"

"I don't know. But I'm not letting her keep my kid from me."

He winces, shaking his head. "I know you've had feelings for Brynne for a long time, but-"

"This has nothing to do with feelings. It has to do with responsibility."

He grunts.

"What?"

"Just don't let her fuck with your head. I care about the girl, too. But she's always had her head stuck up her ass where you're concerned. I don't know why you don't just tell her the damn truth."

"You know why."

"Bullshit reason, bro. You think it's what Sam would have wanted? Her hating you because he was off his meds-"

"Don't."

With a shake of his head, he stands. "I just don't want to see you get hurt…"

I hear the word he doesn't say. *Again.*

"What? You think I should just forget about her, forget

47

that she had my kid? 'Cause there's no way in hell I'm doing that."

"That's not what I meant." He pushes his hair off his forehead before placing his goalie mask back on. "I'm just saying take it slow."

I watch him leave, then mutter under my breath when he's gone, "I've never done anything slow in my life, and I have no intention of starting now."

CHAPTER 6

*B*rynne

I'VE NEVER BEEN a cruel person, or at least I didn't think I was. Not until I saw the look in Kane's eyes when he realized Noah was his.

I'll never forget the betrayal that burned in his gaze, the hurt and confusion. I thought I was doing the right thing by not telling him, but maybe I was wrong.

Maybe you're wrong about a lot of things.

I shake the thought away.

Just because Kane didn't flip out over finding out about Noah, doesn't make him one of the good guys.

I wrap my fingers around my cell phone as I pace my small apartment. I've debated calling him all day. The team will be leaving tomorrow for an away game. I shouldn't care. I went a whole year without seeing him; a few days won't make a difference. I should just let him come to me. I told him my address, so it wouldn't take much investigative work for him to find out what apartment I'm in.

Maybe he won't come. The whole possessive thing at the cemetery was probably because he was drunk. When he finally sobered up, I'm sure he realized the truth of my words. Noah and I are better off without him.

The thought leaves a bitter taste in my mouth.

I walk over to where Noah is sleeping, in the hand-me-down crib I bought from a thrift store, and the bleached-out sheets that once had clowns on it.

It's not the life I want to give him, but I'll make it work. On my own. Because despite what my father thinks of me, I'm not some weak, spoiled little girl who needs her daddy's money to survive.

I'm strong. Stronger than he ever gave me credit for. And I don't need him or Kane interfering in my life. Or my son's. Their world is toxic.

Money. Fame. Those are just the things people see. But what's underneath, hidden from the cameras, is something far less glamorous.

Broken families. Broken promises. Men who think they are gods, who think their actions don't have consequences.

My dad. Kane. They're the same. They're not meant to be fathers. Maybe Kane was smart enough to realize it.

A hard rap on my door makes me jump. I stare at it like it's just sprouted two heads, ready to devour my whole little world.

"Brynne," comes the deep, muffled voice.

It's *him*. I know it. I can practically feel the heat, the tension vibrating from behind the worn out wooden door.

With a shiver, I walk across the room and glance through the peep hole.

Kane stands there, his image distorted by the small piece

of glass, but I can still see the strained lines of his face, and the look of determination in his eyes.

I let out a long sigh and place my forehead and palms on the door.

"I know you're there, Brynne. Heard your damn footsteps. Let me in."

Slowly, I undo the chain and the deadbolt, then open the door, just enough that we're standing face to face.

He's leaning with one palm on the door frame, causing his t-shirt to ride up slightly, exposing an inch of skin above his belt, and the line of dark hair that disappears under the waistline of his jeans.

Shamelessly, my eyes roam down his body.

My heart races, and I feel my ears get hot under his own appreciative gaze. His eyes don't waver. Not for a second.

I pull my bottom lip between my teeth and look away, but I can already feel the heat warming my cheeks, the tingling in my core, the way my thighs clench when his musky scent, a scent that is all Kane, fills my nostrils.

Stupid chemical reaction.

His breath is heavy, harsh, just like his gaze, and I can tell he's trying with great difficulty to hold back his anger.

It's a weird feeling, him being upset with me. Like our roles are reversed.

It's unsettling. Especially since I know I deserve every dagger he's shooting at me now.

"Your boyfriend here?" He glances over my shoulder as if expecting to find someone.

"Felix? I told you he's just-"

"The guy who's been helping you raise my kid," he growls out. "Yeah, I did a little research."

I suck in a breath, more from the hurt I hear in his voice than the anger.

Kane closes his eyes and scrubs his hands over his face,

then through his hair, making the short, dark waves stand on end.

"You're spying on me?"

"Wouldn't have to if you'd be honest for once in your life."

I start to argue, but his look stops me.

"I didn't come here to fight." He lets out a frustrated sigh. "Can I come in?" His jaw is tense, face strained, but he adds, "Please."

I nod and open the door wider, moving back so that we don't touch when he comes into the room.

That's pretty much what the apartment is – one small room that consists of a kitchenette, futon, my art supplies, and Noah's crib. There's a small bathroom with a standup shower, and a single closet for storage. It's smaller than the apartment over my father's garage, but at least it's mine.

If I can find a way to keep paying the rent.

Kane's brows turn down and he frowns as he looks around.

Before he can make some judgmental comment, I snap, "Whatever you're thinking, don't say it. There's nothing wrong with the place. It's clean and safe. Just because it isn't-"

"I'm not here to judge you." His gaze hardens on me. "There's been enough of that."

I open my mouth to answer him with a harsh retort, but clamp it shut when he takes a step towards me, with an expression so feral I swallow back the whimper that forms in my throat.

"For one goddamn second, can you let go of whatever vile, made-up image you've created of me in your head?"

I wish I could conjure that image right now, because as he hovers above me, all six-foot-two of bulging muscles, the only thing I can think about is running my fingers across that broad chest, down his defined abs and narrow hips.

He leans closer, so close I can see the faint scar above his top lip. A scar he got a few years back from a stick to the face.

There'd been so much blood. I shouldn't have cared the way I did. But even from my living room, miles away from him, I'd felt the shot like I'd taken it.

I'd called him that night, admitting that I watched the game. The truth is that I never missed one.

"Careful, Baby Jacobs," he'd slurred, already halfway to intoxicated when he'd answered my call. "You sound like you actually care."

"Don't flatter yourself, Madden." I'd hung up when I'd heard a shrill feminine laugh in the background.

That was the last time I'd ever allowed myself to care.

He's watching me now, the blue of his eyes barely visible past the black of his pupils.

I take a step backwards, and cross my arms over my chest protectively.

"Why are you here, Kane? What do you want? I gave you an out. You can walk away."

He snorts and says sarcastically, "A way out? You really don't know me, do you?"

"Trust me, Kane. I know you better than you think."

"You hate me," he sneers. "And I've let you."

"Let me?"

He gives a harsh shake of his head. "But no more."

"You think you can just snap your fingers and make everything you've done disappear?"

The look he gives me makes me wonder if he thinks he can.

"You're going to have to forgive me for whatever you think I've done."

"Why?"

"Because we have a kid together, Brynne. And I'm *not*

walking away from him." He points his finger at me. "I'll fight you every damn step of the way if you try and keep him from me. This isn't just about you and me, this is about-"

"Okay."

"-him. He deserves a father-"

"I agree."

Kane straightens, looking at me like I'm trying to trick him somehow. "You do?"

I nod. "But there are-"

Noah lets out a quivering cry from his crib.

Crossing the room, I pick him up, shushing and rocking him until he settles. He hasn't been sleeping well lately, which means I haven't been sleeping. My body is tired, my brain is foggy, and some days I'd do anything for a real bath, with bubbles and essential oils, rather than a lukewarm shower.

Kane is behind me, the heat of his body warm against my back. Part of me wants to lean back into him, to feel the strength of his arms around me, even just for a moment.

"Can I...hold him?" Kane asks, his voice cracking with emotion.

I turn and my throat tightens when I see the look in his eyes as he looks at Noah.

"Yeah."

Swallowing hard, I lift him, transitioning Noah into Kane's arms.

Noah's head rests in the crook of his arm, and his eyes widen when he glances up at Kane, one little fist reaching out to touch his face.

"Hey, buddy."

Noah gurgles in response.

Something inside me breaks. Some essential part that's kept me strong over the past months, and I feel a flood of feelings bursting in my chest. The damn bricks I'd built around my heart start to crack.

Danger, my head warns. *It's all a façade.*

This is the same man who spends his money on over-priced booze and cheap women. He's not a good man. Not a man I want my son to grow up idolizing. Which he will. Because if Kane is good at one thing, it's putting on a show.

But the way he stares at Noah with pride and affection, the smile that tugs at the dimples in his cheek, it seems genuine. Real. And in a way, that scares me more than the half-assed, I'll-do-my-part response I'd expected from him.

"He looks like me."

I nod, because there's no denying it.

"I won't hurt him." The words sound forced, and when he meets my gaze I can see the resolve in his eyes. "I won't hurt either of you."

I don't want to believe him.

It's so much easier to hold on to anger and blame.

But deep down, I've always known the truth about Kane. He'd never willingly hurt anyone. The problem is people like him can't help but destroy the people who care about them.

My father is the same.

Bright, blazing stars that can't help but extinguish everyone else's light.

"Did you tell my father?"

Kane's never experienced my father's wrath. Not really. But I know the monster that lives inside the man.

He never raised a fist to me or Sam, but he didn't have to. My father knew how to wield words like a weapon. Words that could destroy and kill.

And in the end, they did.

Kane studies me for a long moment. When he shakes his head, I let go of the breath I didn't know I'd been holding in.

"But you can't keep this from him. *We* can't keep it from him."

I know.

"He'll probably have you traded within the week."

Kane laughs. "Maybe."

His laughter is infectious. It always has been. And I can't help the tug at my lips.

"But honestly, Brynne, I think he'll just be glad to know you're okay."

I don't know how, after all these years, Kane still doesn't see my father for who he really is. Cold. Cruel. With no love for his children.

"If he really wanted to find me, he would have."

Carefully, Kane places Noah back in his crib. "Maybe."

He takes a step towards me, and I take one back, making him shake his head. "Do I really scare you that much?"

"You don't scare me." *Lie.*

He raises an eyebrow. "You're terrified of how I make you feel."

"This isn't about *us*." I take another step back, even though he hasn't moved an inch. But I don't trust myself if he touches me again. "If you really want to be a part of Noah's life-"

"I do. And I will be. That's not up for debate."

My fingers itch at my sides. I ball them into fists, shifting under Kane's gaze, not knowing what to say or do next.

I can practically see the plan formulating in Kane's brain. How he'll get what he wants. What he'll need to do to get it.

"Then I guess we should talk details." I walk over to the miniature fridge and pull out two beers, handing one to Kane when he approaches.

He stares down at it with a frown.

"You can come see him. We'll figure out a schedule-"

"Is my name on his birth certificate?"

Shit. "No."

The muscle in his jaw bunches and flexes, and his lips tighten in a thin line, before he says, "We'll need to fix that."

Which means everyone will know.

"If the media finds out…"

"*When* the media finds out, we'll deal with it."

This is exactly what I didn't want.

"No, *I'll* have to deal with it. You're used to being in the spotlight. That's not my life. I don't want paparazzi waiting outside my apartment to get a shot of The Golden Boy's bastard kid."

"Don't use that word." Anger flashes in his face and he points his finger at me.

I swat it away, then push on his chest, one hand still clutching my beer. "You better get used to it, because if you make your big announcement, they'll be calling him, and me, a lot worse."

He grips my wrists, and leans down so our noses are almost touching. "Not if we're married."

Married. The word hangs in the air between us.

A thrill of excitement mixes with shock. I blink up at him, hating that for even a second I think about the possibility. It's absurd.

"You're kidding?" The words come out shaky and strained.

"No." He wraps his fingers around my beer, and we do a little tug-of-war with it before I finally let go with an exaggerated sigh. He takes a deep swig, then places it on the counter behind me, his body brushing against mine as he leans over.

"I'm not marrying you."

"Why?"

"Because…"

"That's not an answer."

"You can't be serious."

"I am serious." His hands rest on the counter beside me, trapping me. "Very serious."

Once again, my body responds to his nearness. Warmth starts in my core and spreads, and my heart speeds up.

"This is ridiculous. It's not the freaking middle ages. We had a kid together. It doesn't mean we have to *be* together. God, we don't even like each other."

He smirks. "You may hate me, but you still like me."

"That doesn't even make sense." *But it's the truth.*

"Admit it. You care about me. You always have."

"No. I. Don't." I shove his chest, trying to ignore the ache in my core when my palms press against the hard muscles that ripple under my touch.

"Yes." He rests his forehead against mine. "You." His breath warm against my lips "Do."

"Lust isn't like." My voice is strained, my breathing speeding up, and once again I'm unable to control my body's response to him.

"So, you admit you want me?" He grins again.

The man is infuriating.

"Admitting I find you attractive doesn't help our situation. And it definitely isn't grounds to get married."

"Then move in with me." He holds up his hand when I start to protest. "And before you say anything, I'm not offering because I don't think you can take care of yourself. I want to be close to him. Involved. Not some absentee dad who only gets to see his kid every other weekend."

I sigh. "That's not a good idea."

"Why?"

"Because it'll just complicate things."

"Things are already complicated."

I shake my head. "You know what I mean."

"You're worried about us having sex."

"No." Again, I push against his chest. He doesn't budge. "Maybe. Yes. I don't know. Would you just stop touching me for one second so I can think?"

"I'm not touching you." He smirks down at me. "You're the one that keeps hitting me."

"Because you've got me trapped."

"You sure that's the only reason?" One dark eyebrow raises and his lips twitch.

"God, you're so damn arrogant."

He lets out a small chuckle as he pushes off the counter, then raises his hands as if in surrender. "Okay, I'll behave."

"You've never behaved a day in your life," I mutter, feeling the loss of his heat the moment he steps away.

He chuckles. "I'll make you a promise. If you agree to move in with me, I'll keep my hands to myself." His head tilts to the side, a wicked, dark promise dancing in his eyes. "Until…"

"Until what?"

"Until you beg me not to."

I snort. "Not going to happen."

He shrugs. "Then you have nothing to worry about."

I have everything to worry about.

"Move in with me. Let me take care of you and Noah."

"If you're trying to pull some hero crap, I don't need your help."

"Didn't say you did. But it's still my responsibility."

Since when does Kane Madden care about responsibility?

My head is pounding. I rub my temples and let out a breathy sigh.

I hate him.

The thought doesn't hold the same potency it used to. And no matter how hard I try to stir up that familiar feeling, it's muted by the fact that the man standing in front of me is the father of my child.

How the hell am I supposed to hate him now?

"I can't," I mutter, more to myself than to him. "It's a terrible idea."

"Give me one good reason why."

"I can give you a hundred. For starters, we can't even be in the same room without arguing. And how weird is it going to get when you start bringing women home, or when I-"

A low growl vibrates in his throat. "I think we have enough to deal with without bringing other people into it." Something dark crosses his expression when he says, "Unless you're already involved with someone. You seemed pretty friendly with that guy yesterday."

Again, with Felix. If I didn't know better, I'd think he was jealous.

"He's just a friend. He was there for me when I didn't have anyone else to turn to."

"You could have turned to me." There's a fierceness in his words, the first real hint of anger he's shown. "You *should* have turned to me."

Swallowing hard, I know he's right. "Yeah. Maybe I should have. But…"

I clamp my mouth on all the excuses I've created. The real and imagined ones.

He takes a step towards me and reaches out like he's going to touch my cheek, but he drops his hand before making contact. "Just let me be here for you now."

I hold his gaze, searching for anything that will help me say no. Wanting to see some sort of falseness in him. But the man who stares back at me is someone I've never really seen. Someone devoted, caring, honorable.

Someone that could break my heart.

"I'll think about it."

I can see it's not the response he wants, but he gives a small nod. "Okay."

"Okay," I repeat, suddenly awkward, and not knowing where to go from here.

"I'll be out of town for a few days." He pulls out his keys, twisting a key off the ring, then handing it to me. When I refuse to take it, he sighs and places it on the counter beside me. "You can come by whenever you want. Maybe bring a few of Noah's things for when he stays with me."

Stays with him?

God, I hadn't thought about that. If I don't move in with him, then of course Noah will go to his place, even stay overnight eventually. The thought of being away from him for even a few hours makes my stomach hurt.

"You still have my number?" There's an accusation in the question, but I ignore it.

"Yeah."

"Good. Call me if you need anything," he says before leaving.

What I *need* is to clear my head. Get rid of the ache inside my chest, and the warmer, more pressing one between my legs. What I need is to feel his hands on my body, the strength of his thighs between my own. What I *need* is going to get me in a lot more trouble than I'm already in.

CHAPTER 7

 ane

MY PHONE HASN'T STOPPED BUZZING since I left Brynne's apartment. There's two angry messages from Coach, and a half dozen from Blake and Sebastian both wondering if I finally lost my fucking mind.

Maybe I have.

Asking Brynne to marry me wasn't exactly my brightest moment. Not that I don't want to marry her. God, if the woman had said yes, I'd probably have flung her over my shoulder and carried her down to the courthouse today.

I keep telling myself it's about the kid. That I don't want him growing up without a father around. But I know that's not the only reason.

My impulse control has never been great, especially in times of high emotional crisis.

But it's what makes me the hockey player I am. Quick, snap decisions; they come easy to me. Like I can see the play before it actually happens. And standing there with Brynne inches from me, feeling the heat of her body, seeing the desire in her eyes, feeling her walls finally crumbling - I wanted it. Her. Us. A family.

I rub the back of my neck as I weave in and out of rush hour traffic. I just hope that I didn't scare the shit out of her.

Blake's warning about going slow rings in my head.

Too late for that.

The sun has dipped below the city skyline as I turn the corner towards the underground parking lot of my apartment. With my brain a clusterfuck of thoughts, I don't see the small form that steps out of the shadows as the garage door slowly lifts until she's standing a couple of feet from my door.

Hoodie pulled over her head, and tangles of long, matted blonde hair fall over her pale face.

She approaches the car slowly. I don't see one of those cardboard signs, but I have no doubt she's looking for me to give her some spare change. I'm surprised security hasn't removed her. We don't get a lot of beggars in this neighborhood, but the ones we do are usually escorted quickly back to their own side of town.

The girl keeps walking closer as I pull up the garage door and wait for it to open for me. I'm about to drive by, ready to give the front desk shit, when I catch the girl's eyes - blue, desperate, and all too familiar.

Shit.

She starts to retreat into the shadows as I put the car in park and open my door.

"Kiley?"

She stops, but her gaze darts around us, as if she's already plotting an escape.

When the girl showed up at my apartment eight months ago, claiming she was my sister, I figured she was just some chick looking to piggyback on my success. Even if she was related to me, I wasn't sure I wanted anything to do with that part of my life.

She'd sworn she didn't want anything from me. Not that I believed her. Still, I'd had my lawyer dig into her past. Find out who she really was. If she was going to be trouble. Because as much as the media loved a success story, they loved dirt even more.

But by the time I realized she was who she said she was, she'd disappeared. And the number she'd given me to reach her had been disconnected.

Seeing her now—dirty, skinny, and haunted—I swear I see my mother standing in front of me. Or, at least, what my eight-year-old brain remembers of the woman who'd given birth to me. Because that's how old I was the last time I saw her, when Child Protection Services removed me from her care and tossed me into the foster care system.

I know some kids go looking for their birth parents. Not me. I wanted nothing to do with the woman who neglected me, who'd used our government subsidy for drugs rather than food. And I sure as hell didn't want anything to do with the asshole who'd shown up once every couple of years to beat the shit out of the two of us, before leaving again.

People talk a lot of crap about foster families, but I was lucky. The Hilliers took me in, and they fought to keep me. They were never able to officially adopt me, but they were my parents in every way that mattered.

Kiley wasn't as fortunate.

I don't know much about her past, other than she was sent into foster care when she was still in diapers. But unlike me, she flipped from family to family until she finally aged out of the system last year.

She picks at her nails and fidgets, looking like she's ready to bolt at any second. The last time I saw her, she'd been wearing the same torn jeans, same black hoodie, but at least then they'd been clean.

"I know you told me not to come here," she stutters, glancing around nervously, and I can see the small tremor that causes her hands to shake. From drugs, lack of food, or both, I don't know. But one thing's for sure, she's in trouble. "But, I..."

I don't know the girl. Other than sharing the same DNA as a deadbeat junkie, we have no connection. But I can't ignore the nagging pressure at the back of my skull that she's my responsibility.

Shit. I have too much going on right now to deal with another addict. And, in all honesty, getting pulled back into that world scares the shit out of me.

"What do you need?"

She chews on her bottom lip and gives a small shake of her head. "I'm...just late on this month's rent. I know I told you I didn't want any money, and I don't. But..."

"How much?"

"Five hundred. I'll pay you back. I swear."

How many times had Sam said the same thing? I never saw the cash. Not that I expected to. I didn't give two shits about the money I gave him.

And if I didn't think the girl would race off to her dealer for another hit of whatever she's on, I'd give her whatever she asked for.

"You using?" I have to ask it, even though I already know the truth. The dark circles under her eyes, her thin, almost frail features, the way her clothes hang off her body - the trembling. I know the signs.

"What?" Her already too big eyes widen, then she shakes her head. "No. This was a bad idea. I should go. I'm sorry for bugging you."

She starts to walk away, and I curse under my breath.

"Kiley, wait."

Hands tucked into the front pocket of her hoodie, shoulders slumped forward, she turns slightly so I can only see half of her face, but what I do see guts me – humiliation, pain, fear.

"Come inside. I'll order us something to eat. You can get cleaned up-"

"I can't," she mumbles. "I have to be at..." Her mouth clamps shut on whatever she was going to say.

A car pulls up behind mine, and gives a small honk when I don't move.

Fuck.

I pull out my wallet. Two hundred bucks. That's all I have on me.

"Here." I hand her the money, and when she doesn't take it, I grab her hand and place the bills in it. "I'm away for a couple days. Come back on Tuesday and we'll talk. I'll get you whatever you need."

The horn blares again, this time longer.

I glare at the guy before turning back to Kiley. "We'll get you the help you need."

"I'm not a junkie." The words are whispered, her voice faltering.

Another honk. This time, I turn and give the guy the finger. "Two fucking minutes, man."

But when I turn back, Kylie is disappearing around the corner.

I doubt she'll come back.

And maybe it's for the better.

Even as I think it, I know I'll regret not trying to get more information out of her. The girl is on a one-way train to fuck-up-ville, and as much as I'd like to help her, I learned the hard way that you can only help people who want to be helped.

CHAPTER 8

rynne

I sɪт on my lumpy futon with Noah in my lap, and he gives me a big toothless grin when I tickle his belly. I laugh with him, which only makes him giggle harder.

The hockey game plays softly in the background, as it always does when the Annihilators play. Even when I was in Europe, I'd stay up late or wake up early, depending on the time, and stream the games.

I don't know why I watch. But I do. Like a bittersweet torture that I can't turn off.

"That's your Grandpa," I mumble against Noah's head when the camera zooms in on my father's face, which is bright red from screaming at one of the refs.

I know that look well. The deep baritone that could, and has, made grown men cry.

At home, his anger was usually directed at Sam. Usually for something he did that didn't live up to the great Steve Jacobs' expectations. We were always a disappointment. Neither of us could do anything right in the man's eyes. Especially Sam.

My stomach does a little flip when Kane stands up on the bench and says something in my father's ear. My dad gives a sharp nod, then slaps Kane on the back, before sending him onto the ice.

The two of them have always had a connection. An ease of talking. Maybe it's because they're so similar.

Hard.

Focused.

With one love – hockey.

"For someone who claims to hate the sport, you sure watch a lot of it," Felix says, shifting two bags of groceries in his arms as he comes into my apartment.

I frown when I look over at him. I wasn't expecting him to come by tonight. And I don't like that he thinks he can come in without knocking. It's the second time this week. I keep forgetting he has a spare key. I gave it to him when I was in the hospital after I'd had Noah. He'd used it to pick up a few things for me. But he'd never given it back.

"I told you I don't need you to bring me groceries."

"I know." He pulls out a bag of tomatoes and places them on the counter. "But it's Saturday night. I'll make dinner." He holds up a bag of spaghetti and winks. "Then we can watch a movie when Noah goes down."

Definitely time to put some boundaries up.

I place Noah in his swing, then give it a crank, before standing.

Felix already has the cutting board out and is starting to peel the garlic bulbs when I walk over to him.

"I'm actually pretty tired tonight."

He pulls out a knife from the drawer and starts dicing the garlic.

"If you're worried about falling asleep during another movie, I'm getting used to it." He winks at me again, a grin tugging at his lips, then he nods at the bag beside him. "Can you wash the red peppers?"

I sigh and grab the bag, taking it over to the sink.

Felix has been a good friend, and I don't want to seem ungrateful. But I'm starting to get the impression that he wants more than just friendship.

I assumed that me having a kid was a big, blaring red light. But maybe I was wrong.

"Kane came by last night," I say, handing him the washed peppers.

He doesn't look at me, but I see the muscle in his jaw twitch. "Let me guess, he offered you money to keep quiet about it?"

I don't miss the hostility in his voice.

"No." I lean against the counter and rub the back of my neck. "He wants to be part of Noah's life."

He grunts and shakes his head.

"He seemed sincere."

He gives me a sideways glance. "And you believe him?"

"I don't know. But he wants me to move in with him."

Felix stops chopping, his fingers going white around the knife before he places it on the chopping board. "And?"

"And what?"

"Are you considering it?"

I shrug.

"I thought you hated this guy."

"I do...I did." I rub my palms on my jeans. Even though the volume is low, I hear Kane's name from the television announcers, and when I glance over, I see his face briefly enlarged on the screen before the shot goes back to the full rink. "It's complicated."

"Shit." Leaning against the counter, he shakes his head. "You're really thinking about it?"

"Maybe."

"Do you need money? If you're struggling, I can help."

"No. You've already helped enough. You've been a good friend-"

"Right." He snorts through his nose, and says sarcastically, "A good friend."

"Why don't we make dinner, then we can-"

"You know what? I'm not feeling too great. I think I'm going to pass tonight." He starts towards the door.

"Felix."

He turns, his dark eyes suddenly fierce. "What?"

"I just...I don't want you to be angry with me."

"I'm not angry with you. I'm angry at myself for being a fool, thinking..." He shakes his head, jaw clenched, lips pressed in a thin line. "Just don't expect me to be the guy you go running to when everything falls apart. Because it will, Brynne. A guy like Kane Madden is trouble."

"You don't know him."

His brows pinch down even further. "I know what you've told me. He's bad news. After everything he did to you, you're just going to let him waltz back into your life. Into Noah's life?"

"People make mistakes-"

"You're defending him?"

"No. I just..."

"God, you're in love with him, aren't you?"

"I'm not." *I hate him.* But the thought doesn't hold the same fuel it used to. "He's just...we're just..."

"Just what? Because I'm pretty sure you weren't going to say *friends.*"

No, Kane and I have never been friends. The only thing we've ever had in common was Sam. And now Noah.

Felix sighs heavily, the sound full of resignation. "Just think hard before you decide anything."

I nod and he starts to turn, but when he reaches he door, he stops with his hand on the knob. He glances over his shoulder, his dark eyes burning with something I only now recognize - desire. And I feel foolish for not seeing it before.

"I didn't mean what I said." His jaw ticks, and his nostrils flare. "I'll be here. When he fucks up. When he breaks your heart...again. I'll be here."

"This isn't about my heart. It's about Noah."

His lips twitch up and he gives me a look that says he doesn't believe me.

And, in all honesty, I don't believe it myself. My heart has always been involved when it came to Kane, which is why I'd created a very high, very wide barrier around it.

I know Felix is right.

Given the chance, Kane will destroy me. Just like he destroyed the only person in this world who ever cared about me.

CHAPTER 9

Two Years Ago...

ane

"Can't live like this anymore." Sam's voice is hollow, and I can tell he's on something.

"Where are you?"

Silence.

"Sam. Where. The. Fuck. Are. You?"

"Doesn't matter. I'm already gone."

"What the fuck does that mean?"

More silence.

I grab my car keys, then slam my apartment door behind me before racing towards the elevator, jamming my thumb at the button multiple times as if it'll make it come faster.

"Sam?" I bellow into the phone.

"Yeah, I'm here."

But he's not. Not really. His mind is messed up, and not

just from the drugs. Even when he's not on anything, which isn't often anymore, he's been saying some pretty weird shit.

"Where are you?"

"Apartment."

"I'm on my way over." In the parking garage, I put my car in reverse, squealing the tires. "Just don't do anything stupid before I get there."

"Too late." The words are heavy, like he's fighting off sleep.

Fuck.

"What did you do?"

"Love you, man." His breath comes out in a wheeze. "Take care of Brynne for me."

"Don't fucking put that shit on me. You're going to be fine. Tell me what you took. I'm hanging up. Calling an ambulance-"

"She's always cared about you. And I know..." He sounds so fucking tired, like every word is strained. "I know you love her. It's bullshit you never did anything about it."

"I'm hanging up now. I'll be there soon."

As soon as I end the call, I dial 911.

I'm not a religious person, never have been. But I pray to any God who'll listen to make me get to him on time.

The elevator in his shitty apartment is out of order. I take the stairs two at a time until I reach the seventh floor.

I bang on the door. "Sam, open up."

No answer.

Fear strangles me.

"Open the fucking door."

When he doesn't respond, I step back and slam my heel against the door. The old wood splinters slightly, but doesn't budge. I kick four more times before the old hinges give in.

Sam's lying on the couch, face pale, eyes closed, the needle still stuck in his fucking arm.

I scramble over the fragmented door, bile burning my throat.

Grabbing his shoulders, I shake him hard. His eyes stay closed.

"Come on, asshole. Don't pull this shit on me." I hold his face in my hands and yell at him. His skin is cool, the sockets of his eyes so sunken they look black, and his lips are a disturbing shade of purple.

No. No. No.

"You're dying on me, fucker." I slap him hard. "Wake up."

Still, nothing. Where the hell are the paramedics? They should be here by now.

What do I do?

Check if he's breathing. The thought slams into my skull, breaking something inside me. Because I already know the truth.

He's gone.

I place two fingers on his neck, pressing down, praying for even the faintest pulse.

Nothing.

"Damn you, Sam," I cry, trying to remember the basic CPR training I'd received. I press my palm into his chest and press over and over again. *One. Two. Three. Four...*

I tilt his chin back, opening his mouth, and breathe.

"Come on." I start compressions again.

I don't know how much time goes by. Seconds. Minutes. Hours.

There's a commotion behind me. People coming out of their apartments, whispering, watching, but no one comes to help.

"Sir, you can step back now," someone says, as another person takes over my compressions.

The room spins. I blink and time speeds up, then slows down, like a horrible movie playing violently in front of me.

The paramedics work. They've got their paddles out, and when they press it against Sam's bare chest, his body jerks. For a moment, there's hope.

I hold on to that moment, even when I see the small shake of the paramedic's head.

A roar sounds in my ears, screaming that this isn't happening. It's just a nightmare. One I need to wake up from, *now*.

"Sir?" Someone is talking to me. The paramedic. A man in his early forties, and there's sympathy in his eyes when he places his hand on my shoulder. He keeps talking, but I don't hear his words. The only thing I hear is, "I'm sorry."

My back hits the wall and I sink to the floor, my legs giving out on me as I watch them place him on the stretcher.

I'm numb. Frozen. Can't breathe. Can't think. The only thing that jolts me out of my black hole of misery is the small, strangled cry from the door.

Brynne stands there, looking like she just crawled out of bed, still wearing pajama bottoms and an oversized sweatshirt. She doesn't see me. Her gaze, wide and desperate, is focused on her brother's lifeless body.

She sways like she's going to pass out.

I push myself off the floor, ready to grab her, but she's already staggering over the broken door towards his body.

"Sam?" She pushes past the paramedics, dropping on his body, and I see her flinch when she touches him. "No."

The older of the two paramedics places a hand on her shoulder. "Miss-"

"Why aren't you helping him?" Her eyes are wild now. "Help him!"

"I'm sorry. He's-"

"No." She staggers away from him, swaying again.

This time, I'm there. I clutch her elbows, holding her steady.

She looks up at me, and I can tell it's the first time she's seen me. "Kane? Tell them to help him."

I give a small shake of my head, grief squeezing my chest so hard I feel like my heart is going to explode.

"He's gone."

She tries to pull away, but I hold her, wrapping my arms around her small frame, and trembling when I feel rather than hear her sob against my chest.

"He…he called me." Her hands ball into fists in my shirt. "I was just talking to him. He sounded…wrong."

Fuck, Sam. You selfish piece of shit.

He had to know she'd come. That she'd find him like this.

I keep my hand on the back of her head, pressing it against my chest, so she doesn't see when the paramedics place the white sheet over Sam's face.

One of the paramedics is talking to me, something about making a statement to the police, something about the drugs.

"Yeah, sure, whatever," I mumble, holding Brynne tighter.

I feel her tense in my arms.

"You were with him." It isn't a question. She pulls back, and when she glances up at me, there's accusation in her gaze. "This was you."

I let my hands drop to my sides when she twists away from me, her eyes darting around the room, taking in the drugs that still litter the coffee table. The syringes and pills. Some black tarry substance, and a bag of weed. Fuck, I don't even know what half the shit is. But I know it's bad.

"Brynne," I drag my fingers through my hair. "I'm sorry-"

"Sorry?" She hits my chest, tears streaming down her cheeks. "You think getting high is some sort of game? You killed him. It should be you laying there, not him."

One of the paramedics looks over at me with raised brows.

"Stop it." I grab her arm and force her to look at me. "Do I look fucking high?"

She glares at me, and I know that no matter what I say, she'll see what she wants. Anything to take the blame off Sam for being a fucking coward.

He could put on a good face, especially for Brynne. When she was around, it was probably the only time I saw him sober.

I'd warned him repeatedly not to keep messing with this shit. Even told Coach about it. Begged them both to get him some help.

When he didn't, I pulled away.

Yeah, I was a shitty fucking friend. But I couldn't watch as he destroyed himself.

Maybe if I'd been around more. If I'd pushed him into rehab. Maybe I wouldn't be standing here watching as the emergency crew carry his lifeless body out the door.

Eyes red, face swollen, Brynne glares at me with all the hatred I feel for myself. I know what she's doing, using anger as a shield to protect herself from the grief that could drown her if she let it.

I could defend myself. Scream back. Tell her I'd hadn't been part of the crazy shit Sam was always involved in. That it was him, not me, that bought the cocaine the night she'd seen us. That I'd never touched the stuff – ever.

But I don't.

Because I know whatever I say, she'll never believe me.

She *needs* to make me the villain, because in her eyes Sam could never do anything wrong. Not even when he was higher than a kite, and pawning her things for drug money.

If I didn't give a shit about her, maybe I'd fight her on it. Make her see that I'm not the bastard she thinks I am.

But the warped thing about this whole mess is I do care. Too damn much.

CHAPTER 10

Present

rynne

THIS IS A BAD IDEA.

Those words roll through my head as I ride the elevator up to Kane's penthouse.

The last time I'd come here, I'd been drunk on cheap wine, and allowed my body to rule my actions. Now I'm going back, and all I can think about is his offer. *Move in with me.*

"Bad idea," I mutter, glancing down at Noah, who's fast asleep in the stroller.

I want to hold on to the hate that used to protect my heart, but when I look at Noah, it's hard to remember anything but that night. Not just his touch, but the way his eyes seared my soul. The way he made me feel like he was a part of me. That he was my future, and not a demon from my past.

I hated him.

I loved him.

Stupid emotions that warred constantly against each other.

My stomach twists and my palms sweat as I get off the elevator and stand in front of his door.

It's not just me I have to think about anymore.

Kane was right. Noah deserves a father. And if he's really serious about being part of Noah's life, then I have to give him the opportunity. One chance. I'll give him that.

I knock.

"It's unlocked," comes the deep, muffled reply.

I open the door, wheeling the stroller into the large foyer that currently looks like Babies-R-Us exploded in it. Opened and unopened boxes are piled halfway to the ceiling.

"Kane?"

"In here," he calls out.

I follow his voice to the living room, where he's kneeling, shirtless over a series of large plastic pieces that I'm assuming will be a toddler-sized playset, with a mini-slide and climbing wall built in.

"What is all this?"

He gives me a crooked smile that cuts deep dimples into one cheek. And there go the butterflies again.

"I wanted to be prepared for when you-" He rubs the back of his neck. "When *he* sleeps here. So, I went online and purchased a few things."

I glance at the boxes scattered everywhere. "Did you order the whole catalogue?"

He grins and puts down the screwdriver in his hand, then stands and walks towards me. My heart flutters as he approaches, but like he promised, he doesn't touch me. Instead, he bends down over the stroller to look at Noah.

"He just fell asleep. Don't wake him unless you want to be the one getting up with him in the middle of the night."

"Already told you I did." He straightens, then shoves his hands in his pockets. "He's still not sleeping through the night?"

He says it like he actually knows something about babies, which irritates me.

"Most nights he'll sleep eight hours. But if he doesn't have his full afternoon nap, then he'll fall asleep again after dinner, which means-"

"He'll wake up in the middle of the night. Got it." He winks.

I roll my eyes at him, then nod at the plastic playset he'd been working on. "You do know that it'll be at least a couple of years before he can use most of this stuff? And where are you going to put it? You don't have a yard."

"I've got someone coming to pick up the pool table tomorrow. I'm going to turn the game room into a playroom."

"You love that pool table."

He shrugs, making the muscles in his chest and shoulders bunch. "Kid's got to have a place to play."

I frown. "You don't have to do all this."

He holds my gaze, and I swear I can see the wheels spinning behind his eyes.

"What?" I ask, hoping there aren't any more surprises lurking around the corner.

"Is he okay there for a second?"

I glance down at Noah, and nod.

"Good. I want to show you something."

Stomach flip flopping, I follow him down the hall, wishing he'd put a damn shirt on.

"If you're taking me to your bedroom, I told you, it's totally not happening."

He stops, giving me a mischievous grin that says he doesn't believe me for one second, but when he opens the door we're standing in front of, my mouth drops open.

The entire room has been converted into a nursery. Crib. Change table. Stuffed animals. Even a damn diaper genie.

"The walls still need to be painted. Haven't really used this room, so it's pretty bare."

"It's perfect." Uneasiness settles in my chest, and I don't know why. Maybe because I know I'll never be able to give all these things to Noah.

"There's more. Come on." He takes my hand and pulls me to the next room. "I had it made up for a guest room, but I don't have a lot of guests. It's yours."

I don't go into the room. Can't. I can barely breath as I take in the sleek furniture that's been decorated with silvers and purples. My favorite colors. Everything about it is – *me*.

Overwhelmed doesn't even begin to describe the way I feel. It's too much. Too quick.

"Kane-"

"Before you say no, take a look at this." Again, he takes my hand and drags me to another room, this one with floor-to-ceiling windows with a view overlooking the city.

Weights and workout machines line the walls.

"A workout room. Now that is a bonus," I say sarcastically, since he knows full well I've never exercised a day in my life.

He chuckles. "It's your studio."

I try to keep my expression neutral, but it's hard to hide the way my heart beats a million miles a minute. I didn't expect this. Any of it.

"My studio?" My voice cracks on the words.

"I'll have my people put this stuff in storage, and you can

move your supplies in." He leans against the doorframe, watching me. "What do you think?"

What do I think? That everything is moving at warp speed.

"I don't know. It's…a lot."

He leans closer, and I can smell his aftershave, the tang of mint on his breath. His eyes, clear and blue, stare down at me with an intensity that goes straight to my core.

Bad idea.

"We can make this work, Brynne. Move in with me."

I hold his gaze, while he waits for an answer.

Noah's cry saves me.

"I'll get him." Kane reaches out and brushes his thumb along my jaw, already breaking his own rule. But I can't help but lean into his touch, to crave more.

Yeah, really bad idea.

"Stay here and think about it." He disappears down the hall, towards the now desperate squawking.

A few seconds later, Noah's stops crying.

I glance around the large room with its hardwood floors and bare walls. Even when I lived with my dad, despite the enormous house and multiple rooms, I never had anything like this. Nowhere other than my bedroom to work on my paintings and sculptures.

My father did everything he could to crush my love of art. I didn't understand it then, and I still don't now. When I'd asked to sign up for art classes, he'd put me in hockey, then soccer. And when it was clear I wasn't a team-sport person, he registered me for gymnastics, then ballet, and finally karate.

I did them all. Never complaining, but never really enjoying them. My fingers itched to create, to draw and paint.

"You need to keep your body active," my father would say whenever I'd grumble about going to whatever activity he was dragging me to. "All that artsy stuff just makes your mind weak. Are you weak, Brynne?"

That was one of his favorite questions to ask Sam and I.

"No, Daddy." I shoved back the tears, never understanding why he wouldn't look at my drawings, or why he got mad whenever he caught me doodling in my books.

I learned to hide my drawings from him. Even when the teachers at my school commented on my work, suggesting that I had *real talent*, I didn't tell him, afraid of his anger, his disappointment.

And then I found *the room*. I was eleven. One of the housecleaners must have forgotten to lock it, because I'd never seen the door open before.

It was small, but it had large windows on two sides that were covered by thick, dark drapes. Different sized canvases perched against the wall, some finished, some half started. But it was the easel in the center, with its large blank canvas that drew me. An old palette with crusted paint sat on a table beside it, along with an assortment of different sized brushes. Tubes of half used oils beckoned me, tempting me with their bright colored labels.

Maybe I should have known better. But some part of me wanted to believe that the room was a gift from my father. The paints. The brushes. Secret treasures that he wanted me to find.

The first stroke of color on the canvas and my heart leapt in joy.

I'd make him a beautiful painting, something he would be proud of.

I'm not sure how long I'd stayed there. Probably hours, because by the time my father found me, he was frantic.

"What the hell are you doing in here?" his voice bellowed.

I jumped, smudging an ugly red line across the field of roses I'd created.

"I-I was painting."

He barreled across the room, large and intimidating, and grabbed the paintbrush out of my hand, tossing it across the room. "Who said you could come in here?"

"I…the door…it was open…I thought…"

His eyes filled with more anger when he glanced at the painting I'd done. "Go to your room. Now."

"Daddy, please, I-"

His large hand wrapped around my arm, pulling me roughly from the stool I'd been sitting in.

I cried out at the pain, but he only tightened his grip, his eyes dark and scary.

It's the first time I'd seen that look directed at me and not Sam.

"Go. To. Your. Room." His fingers tightened, pinching my skin, before he finally released me.

Tears blurred my vision as I'd scurried to my room.

Hours went by.

I wasn't called to supper.

When the moon was high in the sky, and the lights under my door went dark, I knew he wasn't coming. There was no explanation. No apology. No comfort. Just silence.

Two days later, I walked by the room again. But this time, the door was wide open and it was empty.

No paints.

No canvases.

No easel.

Just a bare room.

He'd thrown everything away. Even the painting I'd poured my heart into. That hurt more than the bruises that still shadowed my arm.

"You okay?" Kane is standing in the doorway with Noah over his shoulder, blue eyes drawn and filled with concern. "I was talking to you. Didn't seem like you heard me."

"I was just thinking."

"About how much you want to move in here?" His lips twist up on one side.

I can't help but smile at his persistence.

It would be nice to have my own space to paint.

Not a reason to sell your soul to the devil, Brynne.

A devil with piercing blue eyes, lips I want to devour, and abs that beg to be licked.

I sigh. "If we do this-"

His smile stretches across his face, eyes glittering, and I know he thinks he's won.

Damn him. Maybe he has.

"*If* we do this," I say sternly, ignoring the way heat builds in my core when he takes a step closer.

You'd think the fact that he's holding Noah would squash all temptation, but seeing the two of them together only intensifies the desire that simmers inside of me.

He draws closer, and I lose whatever I was going to say.

"If we do this," he repeats with a smug smirk.

"No touching."

"Unless you beg." He winks.

I roll my eyes. "I mean it."

"So do I."

We hold each other's gaze, and I know it's a battle of wills. Who will look away first? Who will cave? But I can't let him win this. I need him to know I'm serious.

"All right." He doesn't look away, but I can tell he's backing down. At least for now. "No touching. Any other rules?"

"No random girls coming into the apartment. No parties. And no drugs."

His eyes twitch and his mouth thins. "Not a problem," he says tightly.

"Good. Then we might be able to make this work."

He gives a tight nod, but something has changed in his mood. "I'll have your stuff brought over tonight."

"Tonight? You're not going to be able to get movers on that short of notice."

A touch of a smirk plays on his lips. "Already hired them."

He turns and walks out of the room, murmuring something to Noah.

I follow after him. "And what if I'd said no?"

"You wouldn't have." He chuckles.

I'm about to argue with him, take back our deal, when I hear Noah's own giggle as he reaches out and grabs at Kane's mouth.

Kane turns, his eyes wide. "Did you hear that?"

"Yeah." I heard it. But I'm not sure what made my heart melt more, my son's laugh, or the way his father is looking at him like he's the best thing in the world.

Maybe this won't be the worst decision I've ever made.

Or maybe I'm walking into a trap where I'll be lucky to get out with a shred of my heart left.

Either way, I know my decision was made way before I even walked in the door.

ane

I'VE ALWAYS BEEN an early riser. You get used to waking up before the rest of the world when you play competitive hockey.

But today, it isn't the rush of the game that wakes me.

It's my son's babbling from the room down the hall.

My son.

The sky is still dark as I roll out of bed, then make my way towards his new room.

I heard Brynne up most of the night, pacing the halls, the creak of the bed as she tossed and turned. I'd laid there, listening to her sounds, her frustrated breaths and sighs, wanting nothing more than to go into her room, pick her up, and carry her back to my bed.

"Hey, buddy," I say, glancing down at Noah, who smiles when he looks up at me, arms waving frantically, making more gurgling sounds. "How about we let your mama sleep?"

I pick him up and carry him over to the change table, wincing when I look at the stack of diapers and wipes. I've never changed a diaper in my life. But how hard can it be?

Ten minutes and four failed attempts later, I realize that the bastard who created the damn things must have been a sadist, because every time I pick Noah up, the damn thing falls off.

Noah giggles, pulling his tiny foot to his mouth and gnawing on his toes.

"You think this is funny?"

He laughs again, and I grunt.

"This will have to do." I pray that I've got the damn thing on right. But getting his pajamas back on proves even more difficult. Mostly because I'm afraid of bending his little limbs in the wrong direction, and secondly because every time I try to stick his foot in one leg of the outfit, he kicks his other foot out.

"You're doing this on purpose, aren't you?"

He kicks his legs again, eyes wide and excited like it's all a game to him.

I chuckle. "Okay, no pajamas."

Brynne will probably give me an earful when she wakes up, but the apartment is warm, and there's no chance of him catching a chill.

"So, what next?" I pick him up. His head rested in the crook of my arm, I cradle him like a football against my chest, my heart swelling when the kid looks up at me with those big blue eyes. "I'm thinking you're probably hungry."

There are bottles in the fridge. I heat one up, while still holding Noah. I watched Brynne do it last night. She made it seem easy. Holding the kid in one arm, while doing everything else with the other.

But when I spill the first bottle as I try to test the temperature on my wrist, I start to wonder if she doesn't have superhuman abilities.

Noah whimpers, getting restless in my arms.

"Hold on, buddy. It's coming."

I have better luck with the second bottle.

By the time I sit down on the couch to feed him, the soft glow of the sun is stretching across the city.

I place my feet up on the coffee table as Noah sucks back the bottle, his gaze locked on mine like he's studying me.

"I'm your daddy."

His brows draw up.

I know he doesn't have a clue what I'm saying, but part of me wonders if he doesn't understand something.

"Your mom thinks I'm a bit of a fuck-up. And she's not entirely wrong. I've done a lot of shitty things in my life. Things I wish I could take back. But you're not one of them."

I swear to God the kid stops sucking and smiles. It's just a fraction of a second, but it makes my heart swell inside me. This is good. Better than good. It's perfect. The only thing that would make it better is Brynne. Having her trust me. Wanting the same things I do.

Maybe it's an asshole move manipulating her into moving in with me. But I never claimed to be a saint. And she already thinks I'm the fucking devil.

"I'm going to make this right. You and me, we're going to have to stick together. Make your mom see that we can be a family. I'm going to admit, it's not going to be easy. She's stubborn. Hell, she may just be the most willful, frustrating woman I've ever met. But she's mine. *Ours*. And I'm going to make sure she knows it."

CHAPTER 12

rynne

I WAKE UP SLOWLY, stretching under the soft Egyptian cotton. It took me ages to fall asleep last night. Knowing Kane was just down the hall had my body on edge. And once I finally fell asleep, my dreams were filled with him. His eyes, his touch, his mouth. Even now, I can still feel the phantom pressure in my core. The delicious ache that makes me want things I have no right wanting.

The sun creeps through the thick blinds, and I frown, squinting. I panic when I grab my phone and see what time it is. It's already eight. Noah never sleeps in this late. Ever.

Panic twists in my gut as I jump out of bed and race to his room.

He's not there.

More panic.

"Kane?" My voice is shrill, edged with alarm.

"In here," he answers from the living room.

Kane is spread out on the couch, head tilted forward, eyes closed, with Noah fast asleep on his bare chest.

My stomach does one of those flip-flop things that tells me I'm in way deeper than I should be. But I can't help the way my gaze roams down his body. Sculpted abs, narrow hips, even his damn feet are sexy.

When I look back at his face, I find a pair of intense blue eyes staring back at me, and a grin tugging at his lips.

Busted.

"Enjoying the view?" He cocks a brow at me.

"I've seen better," I lie, turning around so he doesn't see the red that I'm pretty sure creeps into my cheeks. I try to keep my tone stoic, but it comes out sounding bitchy when I say, "You should put him in his crib. I don't want him getting used to being held while he sleeps."

I hear him grunt behind me as I walk into the kitchen and pull out the coffee grinds.

Walls. I have so many of them, especially where Kane is concerned. Instead of being grateful that he let me sleep in, I ended up criticizing what was really a sweet moment.

But the second I let those walls down, I know I'm in even bigger trouble than I'm already in.

No. It has to be this way. At least until I know for sure that this is real. That he's not going to change his mind, or screw it up in the typical Kane Madden fashion.

A few minutes later, Kane comes up behind me, his arm brushing against mine as he reaches past, pulling two mugs from the cupboard.

He doesn't say anything, just leans against the counter, arms crossed over his chest, watching me as I finish pouring water into the coffee maker. I turn around, crossing my own arms.

"You never were a morning person." He chuckles, reminding me of all the nights he used to spend at my house. All the mornings he'd tease me with his overly bright smile.

"There's something wrong with people who can roll out of bed with a smile on their face."

"Trust me, sweetheart. If you were in my bed, you'd be waking up every morning with a smile on your face."

I roll my eyes, but there goes my stomach again with the stupid butterflies.

"Don't you have a practice or somewhere to be?"

"Coach gave us the day off."

I wince at the mention of my father.

"Speaking of Coach-"

"No."

"So, you're never planning on telling him? He's going to find out."

I shrug, turning to fill the mugs with coffee. "Haven't spoken to him since the funeral. Even before that, we barely talked. Me having a kid doesn't change that."

Kane takes the mug from my hand, frowning, before taking a sip. "I'm not hiding this from him. Not hiding my son from the world like he's something to be ashamed of."

"That's not what I'm doing."

"No? You sure about that?" He puts his cup down, the muscles in his arms and chest tense.

I have to look away, the familiar ache warming my core.

"I'm not ashamed of Noah."

"No. But you're ashamed of who his father is."

I glance back at him, and swallow hard when I see the hurt reflected in his hard gaze. I don't deny it, even though I can see he wants me to, even though I know I should. But he's right, in a way. I don't want people to know what happened between us.

I don't want them to know how weak I am when he touches me. Or how my knees tremble when he says my name. And I don't want them to know that, despite how much I've tried to hate the man, my heart has only ever belonged to him.

"Just give me a few weeks. Let's just deal with this for now. See if it's even going to work out before we let the world in on our secret."

His nostrils flare as he exhales, but he gives a curt nod. "Fine. For now, we'll do it your way. Two weeks. Then, we tell your father."

"Three."

"Two. And I'll be the one to tell him. Unless you want to be there."

"Fine. And no, I really don't."

"You're so much like him it's scary. No wonder the two of you butt heads."

"I am *nothing* like my father."

He chuckles, pushing off the counter and taking a step towards me, not touching, but close enough that I can feel the heat radiating off his body, see every detailed muscle in his arms. The way his abs bunch tighter when my gaze drops. The soft brown hairs that sprinkle across his chest, down his stomach, growing darker as they near the waist of his jogging pants.

I swallow hard.

"So damn stubborn," he says, fingers clenching and unclenching like it's taking all his willpower not to touch me.

I know, because I feel the same.

"You say it like it's a weakness." I jut my chin out defiantly. I hate that he thinks he knows me.

"It is when it stops you from taking what you want."

"And what do you think I want, Madden? An arrogant, hotheaded hockey player that can't keep his cock in his pants? Just because I don't want to become one of your little playthings, doesn't make me stubborn. It makes me smart."

93

Instead of arguing back, he just gives me one of his who-do-you-think-you're-lying-to smiles and shakes his head.

"If all I wanted from you was a quick fuck, you'd already be in my bed. I want more. I want everything. Every sexy, willful, damaged piece of you. I know that scares the shit out of you. It scares me, too. But it's happening, Brynne."

My God, the man makes my head spin.

Where are those damn walls when I need them?

"Just remember this a trial. One strike and you're out."

"Pretty sure it's three strikes."

"You've already used up your other two."

"I didn't even know I was up to bat."

I roll my eyes at him. "I'm serious, Kane."

"So am I." His head dips lower.

"This isn't a game."

"Funny, for a second I thought we were playing baseball."

"God, you're infuriating." I smack his chest, but he catches my wrist, holding my palm against his warm, hard flesh.

"Rule number one. No touching." He tsk tsks, shaking his head as his callused thumb runs across my wrist and palm, sending a blast of fire up my arm and straight into my belly. He quirks an eyebrow and a grin pulls at the corner of his lips. "One day, and you're already breaking your own rules. Really, Jacobs, I'm kind of disappointed. I was hoping for a little more of a challenge."

He's teasing me. I know it.

I should pull my hand away, but it's like it's crazy-glued to his damn chest.

Come on, brain, where's my snarky retort? But I can't think of one. All I can think about is the way his heart thumps erratically under my palm. The way his blue eyes practically devour me. Tempting. Teasing. Promising.

My tongue darts out over my bottom lip when his gaze

lands on my mouth, and I know I'm seconds away from kissing him if I don't do something.

"Fine. You win."

He quirks a dark brow.

"You want to do this, let's do it."

"Do what?" His grip tightens around my wrist slightly.

"This. Sex." I place my other hand on his shoulder, dragging my fingernails down his chest, across his abs, then hooking my finger in the waist of his pants.

It's a dangerous game I'm playing. And I don't know what response I'm hoping for.

He groans, deep and guttural.

"Brynne-" My name is a mix between a question and a plea.

"What? This is what you want, right? So, let's do it. Screw the consequences."

He frowns and releases me, taking a step back.

So predictable.

"What?" I bat my eyelashes up at him, stepping closer. "You don't want me if it's not a challenge?"

Raking his fingers through his already disheveled hair, he watches me warily. "I know what you're doing."

I place my hands on his stomach and lean into him, whispering huskily, "I'm giving you what you want. This *is* what you want?"

Push.

Push.

Push.

It's what I'm good at. Pushing buttons. Pulling away. Hiding from anything resembling real emotions.

"You have no idea what I want." His voice is hoarse, clipped.

I glance down at the prominent erection he's sporting and raise my eyebrows. "Clearly, I do."

He takes my hands, threading his fingers between mine.

The gesture is too intimate. "This isn't about sex."

"Of course not." I dig deep inside me and pull out the last remnants of hatred I have towards him, and bite out, "You get a live-in fuckbuddy. I get a place to live. And Noah gets a dad who may be stoned when he comes home after partying with the strippers and puck bunnies that may have given his father an STD." I keep the cold, aloof smile plastered on my face. "Win, win. Right?"

Push.

Push.

Push.

My comment is met with silence. But his eyes say everything, and they call my bullshit.

Yell at me. Fight me. Do anything other than look at me with the pity and understanding I see in your eyes.

He doesn't. Instead, his hands come up to my face, cupping my jaw gently, despite the fierce look he gives me.

"You said no games. So, no fucking games, Brynne. You're hurt. I get it. And you're scared. Me, too. But this is happening. It already happened. You had my kid. You moved in with me. You're *staying* with me. So, drop the fucking act like you hate my guts."

"I-"

His eyes narrow, stopping my words. "You don't trust me. But you will."

And when I do, you'll break my heart.

"I won't," he says as if reading my thoughts. "I won't hurt you. If I do, I give you full permission to cut both my balls off and feed it to the dog."

I can't help but smile at the image. "FYI, you don't have a dog."

He releases me and rubs the back of his neck. "Yeah, about that."

"Uh-uh. No way."

"A boy needs a dog."

"Which boy? You or Noah? 'Cause I know who'll end up taking care of it - me."

He chuckles.

"The rest of your stuff is arriving at noon today," he says, changing the subject and walking to the fridge.

"What stuff?"

"Just some art supplies I ordered." He grabs an apple and tosses it in the air, before taking a bite, then starting to walk away.

"You can't just buy me things."

"That wasn't one of your rules." He gives me a cocky smile.

"It is now."

He shrugs, the muscles in his back flexing and bunching with the movement.

"Oh, and Kane…"

"Yeah?" He glances over his shoulder.

"One more rule."

He frowns. "What's that?"

"Put a shirt on."

He chuckles and turns. "No chance in hell, sweetheart."

CHAPTER 13

 ane

"She moved in?" Blake's mouth hangs open as he leans against the bar, beer bottle frozen in midair.

I don't usually go out drinking after games anymore, but Blake had been bugging me all day about Brynne. And, in all honestly, I hate keeping this fucking secret. I need to talk to someone. Especially since I'll be spending the next few nights alone in a hotel room. Without Brynne. And without my kid.

"Please tell me you didn't ask her to marry you."

I wince, and Blake groans.

"Who's getting married?" A large hand slaps me hard on the back, and I'm greeted by familiar blue eyes.

"Carter 'The Crusher' Bennet," Blake says, standing from his stool and taking the man's hand. "God, it's been a long time. What are you doing here? You still working for that rag piece? 'Cause if you're looking for some good gossip, this guy

—" He shoves his thumb at me and winks, "—has some pretty good shit you might be interested in."

"Really?" Carter's brows go up.

"Thanks, asshole." I glare at Blake, then turn to Carter, shaking his hand. The guy used to be a pretty good hockey player before he busted his knee up. Only played with him a season, but I've seen him around, covering games for whatever paper he works for. "Last I heard, you got yourself hitched and had a kid."

"And one on the way," Carter says, grinning, pulling out his phone and bringing up a picture of a very pregnant brunette holding a little boy.

"Congrats, man. Good looking family."

Blake grunts. "Whatever Kool-Aid you two have been drinking, just keep it the hell away from me."

Carter raises an eyebrow at me. "You had a kid?"

The guy was always one to read between the lines. Guess that's what makes him a good reporter. But the last thing I need is my relationship with Brynne getting out, not without her approval. She'd have my fucking head on a spike.

I take a swig of my beer, before answering. I want to shout it from the rooftops. Show my own damn pictures. But I promised Brynne. I don't know what the hell difference two weeks makes, but I'll give them to her.

Because I know she's terrified. She's one of the strongest people I know. But even steel can bend when put under extreme weight. And these past two years have been a pressure cooker.

"It's complicated," I mutter into my bottle.

Carter leans on the bar, signaling the bartender to bring him a drink. "As in, you don't know if you have a kid, or you don't know if it's yours?"

"As in, he knocked up Coach's daughter," Blake offers, tilting his beer to his lips and draining it.

Fuck, Blake. I want to hit the guy. He doesn't usually drink, but something's eating at him tonight, and it's clear I've got some sort of target on my head.

"Brynne Jacobs?" Carter asks, his eyes going wide.

"One and only," Blake says, as if he's enjoying himself.

Asshat.

Carter whistles. "Damn, Madden. You got a death wish or something? I'm surprised Jacobs hasn't traded your sorry ass."

I glare at Blake, before mumbling, "He doesn't know yet. And I'd appreciate you both keeping your mouths shut about it until I get the chance to talk to him."

Carter nods, but there's something in Blake's eyes that makes me uneasy.

The guy is one of my best friends, and I trust him with my life, but he's got a major stick up his ass right now.

"I mean it, Bennett," I say to Carter. "You can run the story in a few weeks. But I need time."

"Okay." He slaps my back again. I haven't spent a lot of time with the guy, but I trust him.

"Thanks."

Blake is ordering another drink when Carter walks away.

"You going to tell me what your problem is, or am I going to have to beat it out of you? Because, right now, the second option sounds pretty good."

He drains half of the beer the bartender hands him, his jaw clenching, eyes burning with something I can't figure out.

"I'm serious. You can't tell people about Brynne and I. Not yet."

"Fine," he mutters, finishing his beer, then swaying on his stool.

"You're an idiot. You know that?"

He grunts, and we sit in silence for a few minutes while I wait for him to tell me what's really bothering him.

"You hear from Kiley?" he finally asks.

I place my beer down on the bar and study him. He and Sebastian are the only people who know about my sister. I was in a bad place when she showed up. And it was Blake who'd spoken with her. Who'd tried to help her.

I hadn't told him about my last encounter with her because I knew he was already too involved. He always cared too damn much about everyone but himself.

"She came by my apartment a few days ago."

"You saw her?" His gray eyes widen, and there's a hint of anger there, an accusation. "Why didn't you tell me?"

Because it's none of your business. Because the girl is bad news. Because I saw the way you looked at her. Because you're my best friend, and she'll rip your fricking heart out of your chest.

I lift a shoulder, then let it drop. "I only saw her for a minute. Outside the building. She wanted money."

He rubs the back of his neck. "I thought I saw her."

"When?"

"Couple nights back." His knuckles go white around the bottle he's holding. "She didn't look good. But when I called out her name, she looked straight at me, then took off."

I exhale a slow, uneven breath. "She's a junkie. You don't want to get involved-"

"You don't know that."

"I know the signs." I shake my head at him. "Can't go through that again."

"She's your sister."

"Half-sister," I correct. "And until a year ago, I didn't even know she existed."

"That's cold, man."

"No, it's reality. And it's not my fucking problem. You

want to go down to the corner of Third and William and save all the meth heads, be my guest." I push my stool back, knowing I sound like a complete asshole. But I have a family to protect now. "If I thought I could save her, I would. But we both know there's nothing we can do, unless the person actually wants help."

"She's just a kid."

"She's almost twenty." I shift off the stool, ready to go back to my hotel room. "Look. I'm not trying to sound like a dick. If she wants help. I'll be there for her. But I've got Brynne to think about. I'm already walking a thin wire with her, and she's still messed up about Sam. It's just a fucking terrible time to have to deal with this."

He doesn't look convinced. But he's always been a bleeding heart. Always bringing in the strays. Women and dogs. He hasn't had a healthy relationship *ever* because of it.

"Stop trying to fix everyone else's problems, and fix your own."

"I don't have any problems." He lifts his bottle and gives me a forced smile. "Living the dream."

I grunt, pushing away from the bar. "Good, then you can pay for the drinks."

rynne

I WAS WORRIED when I moved in that Kane would be suffo-cating, but with his schedule, he hasn't been around much. The trouble is, when he is around, he's…perfect. *And almost always shirtless.*

I know he's doing it to piss me off, because who the hell walks around without a shirt on all the time? *Kane Madden, that's who.*

Not that I don't enjoy the view. I enjoy it too much. And he knows it.

"Is that supposed to be me?" Kane leans against the door-frame with a smirk, watching me.

I follow his gaze back to the canvas I'd been working on, heat rushing to my cheeks when I recognize the similarities between the male form I'd been sketching, and the man standing behind me.

"Don't flatter yourself."

"If I was, I'd add a little more definition around the abs." He's wearing a t-shirt, a rare occurrence. He lifts it, exposing his stomach, and runs a palm over the perfect six-pack.

I roll my eyes at him. "What do you want, Madden?"

"Noah's asleep."

"Already? But it's only..." I reach for my phone, eyes widening when I see the time.

"Nine-thirty," he says, still grinning. "I didn't want to disturb you."

"Thanks," I mumble.

"I stuck a lasagna in the oven. It should be ready if you're hungry."

My stomach growls. "Starving."

"Me, too," he says, his gaze dark as it roams over my body, then lands hungrily on my lips.

I suppress a shiver.

"Rules," I warn.

"Come on, Jacobs." He grins, then turns. "Time to eat."

I sit down at the kitchen island and watch as he pulls the lasagna from the oven. My mouth waters, and not just for food. But I settle for the lasagna, because as much as carbs are not my friend, they're a lot less dangerous than the alternative.

"It's good," I say, shifting under his gaze.

"Thanks. It's Jane's recipe." I'd only met his foster parents once before they passed away. But they seemed like good people. They had to be for putting up with Kane all those years.

"You made it yourself?"

"You sound impressed."

"I am." My own culinary skills stop short at boiling a pot of water for Ramen Noodles.

He chuckles. "I have a few hidden talents up my sleeve."

"When you wear a shirt," I mumble, making him laugh harder.

"Come on, Jacobs, admit that you love it." He leans on the island, fingers entwined, muscular forearms resting in front of him.

I shake my head, glancing down at my plate so he doesn't see the truth in my eyes. "Just keep your pants on and we'll be good."

He laughs, going to the wine cooler and taking out a bottle of Chardonnay. Pouring two glasses, he places one in front of me.

"I've missed this."

"What?" I take a sip of the chilled wine.

He leans against the counter and takes a sip before answering. "This. *You*. Your snarky comments-"

"I'm not snarky."

"-and the way you watch me when you think I'm not looking."

"I don't."

"You do. You always have." He leans on the island and whispers, "But want to know a secret?"

"No." *Yes.*

"I watch you, too."

"That's not a secret." I take a sip of my wine, trying to hide the warmth that creeps into my cheeks.

Deep dimples cut into his cheeks when he smiles. "No. I guess it isn't. Even Sam knew-"

We both freeze, and he winces.

After a few seconds of silence, Kane takes my plate and places it in the sink.

"Sorry." His back is to me, but I hear the remorse in his voice.

"It's fine. Maybe it's worse if we don't talk about him."

He turns, but there's a wariness in his expression. "Or

maybe it'll just bring up things neither of us are ready to face."

"Maybe." I take a deep sip of my wine.

"He asked me to take care of you." Leaning against the counter, he crosses his arms.

"What? When?"

"The night he died. It's why I knew something was wrong. Hadn't spoken to him in a few months. He'd been..." His voice cracks, his eyes going distant.

He finishes his glass of wine, then refills it.

"I'd been busy. Not an excuse. I know that. Not when I knew he needed help. I did try...once. Took him up to Summerville to the rehab clinic. He was clean for a few months. Thought he was getting better..."

I listen to him. His forced confession. Hear the truth in his words. The guilt.

"You really think he did it on purpose?" I know the answer, but I've never wanted to believe it.

I knew it when he'd called me that night. It's why I'd driven across the city in my pajamas. Praying I was wrong. Hoping I could talk some sense into him.

"He's right, Brynne," Sam had said, his voice void of emotion. "I'm weak."

"Dad's an asshole. He doesn't know you. Not like I do. You're stronger than whatever you're dealing with."

"Love you, dork."

Those were his last words before he'd hung up.

"I just can't believe he'd be that selfish," I say now, running my finger across the condensation on my glass.

"He was struggling with a lot. It wasn't just the drugs."

I narrow my eyes at him. "What else was there?"

He exhales heavily.

"Kane?"

"Does it matter?"

"Yes."

"It doesn't change anything. He's gone."

"And I want to know why. If you know-"

"What? You think it'll make you feel better knowing his secrets?"

"Maybe."

"It won't."

I push off the stool, causing it to screech across the marble floor. "Maybe it's your secrets you don't want me to find out about."

"Right." He chuckles again, but this time there's no humor in it, just bitterness. "Because it's always my fault. FYI, Brynne. I didn't force him to take drugs. I didn't do half the shit you keep telling yourself I did. But you know what I did do? I watched as my best friend slowly, painfully rotted away in front of my eyes because he was too damn afraid to get help. Too afraid to look weak in *your* eyes."

His words slice straight to my heart. Because as harsh as they are, I know there's a sliver of truth to them.

"Fuck." Kane rakes his fingers over his face, then leans with his palms on the counter, back slouched forward in defeat. "I shouldn't have said that."

I sit back down on the stool, my body trembling. "Did he say that to you?"

"No."

He's lying.

I suck in a shaky breath.

"I know you don't want to believe me, but no one except Sam is responsible for what happened. Not you. Not me. *Not Coach.*"

I glare at him. "You don't know what he did. How he treated Sam."

"I was there, Brynne. I saw the way your dad acted around him. Heard the arguments. Sure, he was an asshole, sometimes. And he didn't know how to deal with…" He rubs the back of his neck. "He didn't deal with Sam's illness well. None of us did."

"It wasn't an illness. It was an addiction." I slap my palms on the counter, anger burning my throat. "And he wouldn't have touched the stuff if you hadn't-"

"Screw that," he yells. "You want to blame anyone but the one person you're really angry with."

His breathing is harsh, and so is mine. We stare at each other, anger simmering between us.

"You want me to take the blame?" I ask, my voice hoarse, tears burning the back of my eyes. "Of course, I'm angry with myself. You think I don't regret not being there for him? For missing the signs?"

He moves around the island towards me and pulls me against his chest. "I wasn't blaming you."

I want to hold on to the anger, the hatred that has been my anchor, but it too easily dissolves when he touches me.

He pulls back, cupping my jaw and forcing me to look at him. "You want to be angry at someone, then be angry at Sam."

I hate that he's right.

Heavy arms wrap around me, but I don't want to be held. I don't want his comfort. Or maybe I do. Maybe I'm just so damn scared of what it'll mean if I accept it.

I push him away, but he doesn't release me.

"Be angry, Brynne. But be angry at the right person."

"I can't." A damn sob chokes my words. "I'll never know why he did it. Why he destroyed his life. You think I don't want to be angry at him? I do. But he's not here."

"No. But I am." He cups my face again, his thumbs stroking away the tears that spill over my cheek. "So, if you need to yell or cry, or whatever it is that'll make you feel better, then do it. I'll be your fucking punching bag, Brynne.

Give me your best. But when you're done, you're going to finally admit that you don't hate me."

"I don't hate you," I whisper. "But…"

He rests his forehead against mine. "I'm angry with him, too. Angry with myself. With Coach. But it's time to let it go."

"I can't." Because it feels like I'm letting Sam go if I do.

He exhales, his breath warm against my lips. My body melts into his, and my fists tangle in his shirt.

We stand like that for a long time. I take his strength, his heat, clinging to him.

I should walk, no run, away. But I can't. I don't want to.

"How can something feel so right and yet so wrong at the same time?" I whisper.

"It's not wrong," he breathes into my hair, his palms pressed firmly against my lower back. "I'm not saying it'll be easy, but we'll make this work. We'll make us work."

"There is no us, Kane. It was one night, and-"

"Bullshit." His body tenses, but he doesn't let me go.

I place my hands on his chest and push back. "You really think we'd be standing here right now if it weren't for Noah?"

"Yeah, I do. Maybe not here or now. But we've been fighting this thing between us for too damn long. Sam saw it. You know he did. And he didn't care. You think he'd care now, when we need each other more than ever?"

"I don't need you."

"God, you're so damn stubborn." His mouth crashes down on mine, almost painfully, his kiss filled with a tsunami of emotions.

Despite the warning bells that blare in my head, I kiss him back.

His fingers tangle in my hair, and his tongue darts out against my lips, pushing forcefully into my mouth. Taking. Devouring. It's filled with devastation and ruin. Promising things that we can never be. That neither of us can ever have. At least, not together.

There's too much between us. A chasm of mistrust and misunderstandings.

But he's right. I need him. His body. His touch. And I know I'm seconds away from making the same mistake I made a year ago.

His phone rings on the counter beside us.

He flinches.

"You should get that," I say breathlessly, as his mouth skims frantically across my neck, his hands dropping to my waist, tugging me firm against his hard erection.

"They'll call back," he growls against my ear.

My self-control is a puddle in his hands. "Don't you want to see who it is?"

"No."

I manage a quick glance at the name that pops up.

Coach.

My father.

Ice rushes through me, turning the lava that was pumping through my heart a second ago to stone, and giving me the strength I need to push away.

I reach past Kane and grab his phone, pressing answer before he has a chance to stop me.

"What are you-"

"Hey, Daddy," I say with all the false sweetness I can muster.

"Brynne?" He hesitates, and when he continues, there's uncertainty in his deep baritone. "I thought I called-"

"Kane? Yeah, this is his phone. I'm living with him now."

Kane's mouth drops open, his face draining of color.

"Oh, and we had a baby. Surprise." I hang up, and toss the phone at Kane, which he just barely catches before it crashes to the floor. "Happy now?"

His initial shock lasts about two-point-four seconds, before his face goes from chalk white to blood red. And I swear if we were in one of those cartoons, steam would come out of his ears.

"What the hell did you just do?"

Something I have a feeling I'm about to regret.

ane

MY PHONE STARTS to buzz in my hands and Coach's name is popping up on the screen.

Fuck.

"You should answer that." She crosses her arms, eyes full of stubborn defiance.

"Why would you-"

"You wanted everyone to know." She shrugs. "Now, everyone will."

"Jesus, Brynne." I'm so angry, I don't trust myself to say anything else.

As soon as my phone stops, it starts up again.

I can't ignore him. But I also can't let her get away with her little stunt. I know exactly why she did it. I pushed her too hard. And instead of admitting the truth, that she needs me, she lashed out. Burying us both.

I won't let her get away with it. But right now, I have to

deal with Coach before he ends up at my door, and we have a whole other problem on our hands - me in a seven by two wooden box, six feet under.

She gives me a triumphant smile, then turns and walks away like she hasn't just completely fucked me over.

"We're not done talking, Brynne."

Ignoring me, she walks down the hall towards the bathroom, shutting the door behind her. A few seconds later, I hear the shower turn on.

When the phone starts ringing for the third time, I finally answer it. "Hey, Coach."

I have to hold the phone away from my ear as he screams a string of explicit curses that amount to him wanting to cut my balls off and feed them to my dead whore of a mother.

"To think I trusted you, Madden. I let you into my goddamn house. And this is how you repay me? Sneaking around behind my back. I expect this from Brynne, but you..." His ranting slows, and I can hear the hurt in his voice, the slur of his words. He's been drinking again.

I rub the back of my neck, not knowing what to say. Even the truth sounds like a bullshit excuse.

"She's staying with you?"

"Yeah."

"And she's pregnant?"

"No." I steel myself for his reaction, then say, "She had a baby. A boy. Three months old. I didn't know about him until recently, but he's-"

More cursing. This time, I hear something shatter on the other end of the phone.

I could handle anything but the deafening silence that follows. Long, painful seconds. I wait. I've known the man long enough not to interrupt his thoughts, even if they're devising a plan to get rid of me. Or to see me tied up and gagged at the bottom of the river.

"A boy?" His words slur.

"Yeah."

"What's his name?"

"Noah."

More silence, but I swear I hear the man sob.

"Can I...would she let me see him?"

I don't know.

"I'll talk to her."

He breathes out heavily before ending the call.

I slam my phone down on the counter. Despite how fucking well Coach seemed to take the news, I know once he sobers up, there will be hell to pay, and questions to answer.

Do I think he'll try to trade me? No. Because I know what Coach wants. The same thing I do - *Brynne*. And if I leave this damn city, she's coming with me. Whether she likes it or not.

The little brat thinks she's won.

It's almost comical. Because the thing is, I haven't even started playing.

Game on, sweetheart.

rynne

I BANG my head on the cold tiles of the shower as hot water sprays down my back.

What was I thinking?

I wasn't. That was the problem.

I got scared.

So, I did what I always do. I lashed out. But this time, I went too far.

And I know I'm going to pay for it.

The creak of the shower door makes me jump. I spin around, but when I do, Kane is standing there – naked, with a look in his eyes that cries out for retribution. And I know what he wants – me.

Shit.

He moves towards me like a predator stalking his prey, and places his palms on the tiles behind me. Trapping me.

"What are you doing?"

"I told you, we're not done talking." He leans closer.

My back hits the cold tiles. I think about reaching out to push him away, but I know how that will end. With my palms pressed against his rock-hard chest, and my body melting into a puddle of lava at his feet.

"We can talk when we both have our clothes on." My voice is weak, and even I hear the hint of fear in it.

He chuckles darkly, the muscles in his neck and shoulders tensing and rippling, but he still doesn't touch me. "I prefer this."

"I prefer you not jumping me in the shower."

A flash of anger mixed with lust burns in his eyes as his gaze roams over my body. "Haven't touched you, sweetheart. But I'm going to. And you're going to beg for it. Because you want me."

"You're delusional."

"And you're a terrible liar. You always have been. No more bullshit, Brynne. You're mine. Stop fighting it."

Heavy droplets of water hit his chest, running down his abs, and I can't help but follow their path, swallowing when I catch a glimpse of his hard, heavy erection.

Yeah, I'm totally screwed. Or about to be. And it's my fault. I shouldn't have pushed him the way I did.

I squeeze my eyes shut, but it makes the ache between my legs worse, because my mind conjures up all sorts of filthy images when I do.

"You promised." The words come out as a whimper, a plea.

"I promised you'd beg for my touch. And you will."

A small moan escapes my lips. My body aches, and my pussy clenches.

"All you have to do is say one little word, sweetheart, and I'll ease that pain."

"No."

"Wrong word," he chuckles, raking the back of his knuckles across the swell of my breast, then cupping it. His thumb twirls my nipple and I tremble violently.

"Kane," I moan, my hands rising to his hips. I mean to push him away, but the second I touch him, I know I'm finished. My fingers dig into his skin.

"Closer," he growls against my neck, his teeth raking across the sensitive skin. "Say please."

I shake my head.

"Stubborn," he mutters, his mouth dropping to my breast, taking my nipple between his teeth and sucking hard.

My knees buckle beneath me, but he holds me up, one hand gripping my ass, the other plastered against the wall, his cock pressed against my thigh.

His tongue dances across my breast, teasing, sucking, tasting. Every lick, every nip, tears away at my self-control.

"You're mine, Brynne. Your body knows it." He rises, dragging his thumb across my lower lip.

I know he's right. My body betrays me.

"You're wrong."

"Terrible liar," he mutters, dropping his mouth to mine, his lips slow and seductive.

I have no control over my body. Not the way my hands grip his waist, or how my hips press wantonly against his throbbing cock, or the way my nipples turn pebble hard as they press against his hard chest.

"You'll ruin us," I say harshly against his lips.

His fingers tangle in my damp hair, tugging so that my chin lifts. I suck in a breath, and he takes the opportunity to deepen his kiss. His tongue invades my mouth, hard and demanding.

He kisses me.

Hungry.

Possessive.

Angry.

"The only thing that will ruin us is if you refuse what I can give you."

I wrap my arms around his neck as he lifts me up so that I'm straddling his waist. "An orgasm isn't something to base a relationship on."

He grunts, digging his erection harder against my stomach.

I want him so damn bad, my entire body aches.

"That's not the only thing I plan on giving you." Slowly, almost painfully, he releases me, so that I slide down his body. He presses one last, hard kiss on my mouth, before he takes a step back, erection still straining towards me.

I have to press my palms against the tiles to keep from sinking to the floor.

He opens the shower door and grabs a towel, a smirk playing on his lips.

"Whe-where are you going?"

"Bed."

"You're just leaving?" Disbelief makes my voice raise an octave.

He chuckles. "You can join me. But when do, it's *your* choice."

Damn him.

"Oh, and Brynne," he says when he's by the door, not even bothering to wrap himself in the towel. "You will say please."

ane

I LAY in bed with my arms behind my head, listening to Brynne pace the floor of her bedroom. Every few minutes, I hear a muttered curse.

Stubborn woman.

The caveman part of me wants to go in there, toss her over my shoulder and drag her to my bed. It's where she belongs. Where she'll be eventually. But I want her to choose. To come to me on her own. Only then will I know she's starting to trust me.

Eventually I see the soft light from the hallway dim, and I blow out a breath.

I'm not sure if I expected her to come to me. But I know one thing, I wasn't about to take her in the shower, not when I still saw so much uncertainty in her eyes.

My cock aches. Throbs. I haven't touched anyone but Brynne since last year. Had no desire to. But with her sleeping in the room next to me, my balls are constantly pulled tight against my body.

Not even jerking off helps.

But right now, my hand is the only relief I'll get.

I stroke myself, picturing Brynne's tight little body, the way her nipples pebbled against my tongue, her soft moans that she tried so hard to hold back.

A sound makes me open my eyes - a mix between a gasp and a moan.

Brynne is standing by the door, watching me, eyes hooded. Her tongue darts out across her lips. She doesn't move, just stands there in her oversized t-shirt, her hard nipples poking out through the thin fabric, letting me know she's not wearing a bra.

Jesus, this woman.

It's not the first time I've been caught jerking off, but it's the first time it's ever felt...erotic.

I keep stroking myself, my gaze focused on her, not sure what she wants. That's not exactly true. I know what she wants – *me*. She just won't admit it to herself.

"Wouldn't have taken you for a voyeur, Brynne." My voice is rough, my balls tight against my body, my cock so fucking engorged I know it would take one lick of that sweet little tongue of hers to make me come.

"I..." Her gaze never wavers from my cock.

I slow my strokes and grin. "Do you touch yourself, Brynne?"

Her gaze jerks to mine, eyes wide, and even in the dim light I can see the red that creeps into her cheeks.

"When you come, do you think of me the way I think of you?"

She gives a small shake of her head.

Liar. Even now, her thighs press together. And I have no doubt that if I touched her, she'd be wet and ready for me.

"Have you thought about my mouth on your sweet pussy, pretending it's my tongue and not your fingers as you moan in pleasure?"

She whimpers.

"Or do you fantasize about wrapping that sweet mouth around my cock?" The familiar tingling of my shaft warns me that I'm close to spilling myself all over my stomach.

She doesn't move, doesn't say anything, but I can hear her heavy breaths, fast and uneven. Her fingers are fisted in balls at the edge of her long shirt. I'm not sure she's even aware that she's pulling it up, her knuckles sliding across her thighs.

"Touch yourself, Brynne," I command. I know if I demanded her to come to me she would. But I can see it in her eyes she's not ready. She still doesn't trust me. And when I take her, I want every shredded piece of her heart. "If you won't touch me, sweetheart, then touch yourself."

She does.

I almost come when her fingers dip under her panties and her eyes close briefly.

"Are you wet?" I know she is.

"Yes," she whimpers, licking her lips, her hand starting to move rhythmically in time with my own.

"Tell me what you fantasize about, sweetheart?"

"You," she moans. "Always you."

Finally, some truth.

"Show me. Come for me, Brynne."

I know she's close, I can hear it in her breaths, see it in the dark depth of her pupils. When she lets out a small cry, her body trembling, hips rocking against her hand, my own release spurts across my stomach in a rush that has stars dancing behind my eyes.

"Oh, fuck."

She reaches out for the doorframe to steady herself, legs wobbly.

I roll out of bed, taking three long strides to reach her, then scoop her up against my chest and carry her to my bed.

"Kane, I-"

"Shut it, Brynne," I say, laying down beside her. "I didn't get to fuck you. The least you can do is let me sleep with you."

She lets out a small laugh and shakes her head. "God, you're crude."

"You love it."

"And sticky." Her hands are on my stomach and chest as I lean over her.

I glance down at my abs, the evidence of my orgasm still wet against my stomach.

"Give me your t-shirt." I tug at the fabric.

"No." She holds it down when I try to lift it over her head. "Why?"

"For once in your life, can you not argue?"

She sighs, then lets me take it off her.

I use it to clean myself up, then toss it on the floor before turning and drawing her back against my chest. The only thing separating us is the lacy fabric of her thong.

"What are you doing?" She tenses, and I can hear the tinge of fear in her voice, and I know I'm pushing her boundaries. We may not have had sex, but that was just as intimate.

"Cuddling."

She snorts and tries to twist in my arms, the friction against my cock making it stir again.

I slap her thigh gently. "Stop that, unless you're prepared to have me balls deep in you tonight. I held back twice now. I don't think my self-control will last a third time."

She sucks a breath in and goes still, which gives me the opportunity to wedge my thigh between her legs, and nuzzle my nose against her neck.

"Kane, this isn't-"

"Go to sleep." I place my heavy arm over her, locking her in place.

"You're going to suffocate me." She's still trying to put up a fight, even though we both know I've already won. But I expect nothing less from her.

Slowly, I feel the tension release from her, and she melts against me. Soft and warm. She yawns, and I smile. I press my lips against her bare shoulder, listening to the sounds of her breathing as she drifts off.

"You're kind of ruining your bad boy vibe right now." Her voice is filled with sleep, but even in her exhaustion she taunts me. "Who would've guessed Kane Madden was a cuddler?"

I'm not. Never have been. Never allowed a woman to stay the night, or even in my bed. But with Brynne, I never want her to leave.

rynne

WRAPPED in a cocoon of hard muscle, I don't want to wake up. Kane's warm breath is on my neck, and his morning wood pressed into my backside. He murmurs in his sleep, tightening his hold, and I can't help but smile.

But this is bad.

Really bad.

I roll slightly, peeling his fingers away, which causes him to grumble and turn on his back, placing one forearm over his face. The blankets move with him, exposing his hard, muscular chest, defined abs, and the soft line of hair that trails under the covers.

Dark stubble shadows his jaw, and I itch to run my palm over it.

"You like watching me sleep, Jacobs?" His deep voice makes me jump, and heat creeps into my cheeks.

Exposed.

"Just trying to figure out how someone, even your size, can snore that loudly."

He drops his arm, a grin tugging at his lips, as his sleepy gaze rests on me. "I don't snore."

No. He doesn't. But I'm not going to admit it.

"Like a bear," I say, shifting away from him.

But before I have a chance to get away, he tackles me. His weight presses my back into the mattress as his thick thigh spreads mine. His erection digs into my leg and I can't help but let out a small whimper of arousal.

He doesn't play fair. But then, he never has. On or off the ice, he's ruthless.

"Take it back," he growls into my ear.

"You snore, Madden," I try to keep my tone cool, collected, but even I can hear the desire that burns under the surface of the words, begging him to do something about it.

"No." He nips at my ear. "I." His scruff brushes against my jaw. "Don't."

I open my mouth to argue, but his kiss stops me, stealing any fight I have left.

Lost.

That's how I feel when he touches me.

Consumed.

Fully and completely.

No thoughts occupy my brain, because my senses have taken over. Basic primal urges that leave no space for rational thought.

His scent is intoxicating. All male and musky. A hint of cologne still lingering on his skin.

And the taste of him. God, the taste of him is almost too much. I lick his bottom lip, then tug it between my teeth. He groans and I shudder. His own tongue delves into my mouth, deepening our kiss, making my body ache.

His callused fingers roam across my skin, across my

breasts, stomach, hips, and thighs. He pushes my legs wider with his knee, and his hand moves between us, slipping beneath the thin material of my panties.

I'm wet. Even before his thumb strokes my clit, before he slips a finger inside of me, my body is aching and ready for him.

"God, Brynne. Do you have any idea how much I want you?"

I can feel the evidence of it pressed into my thigh. The scary thing is, I want him just as bad.

A small wail echoes down the hall, saving me from making another terrible choice.

"Shit," Kane breathes against my lips, his hand still hot and heavy against my sex, his forehead resting against mine. "I'll get him."

"No." I squirm beneath him, needing to get free, needing the space to regain my composure. "I will."

Kane falls backwards and lets out another low curse, his gaze trained on me as I gather my t-shirt and pull it over my head.

"You okay?" He grinds out, his concerned tone mirrored in his gaze.

"Yeah," I lie, ignoring his grunt of disbelief as I practically run from the room.

Gathering Noah in my arms, I let out the breath I'd been holding in.

I'm far from okay.

Because I'm falling in love with him.

 ane

My BALLS ACHE as I roll out of bed, almost as much as my fucking chest. Damn heart is beating too wildly, hoping and wanting things I know she's not ready to give me.

I dress, then go to the kitchen to start a pot of coffee. Medium blend with a dash of cinnamon, just like she likes it. Then I pull out the formula and start making Noah's bottle.

My phone vibrates on the counter, and I hesitate before checking it. I have no doubt I'll be called into Coach's office before practice today.

But none of the messages that pop up on the screen are from him. There's one from Sebastian asking if I'm coming over tonight to watch the UFC, and the rest are from Blake, each one more desperate than the last.

Call me.

I'm fucking serious, Kane. Call me now.

Get your head out of your ass and return my call, dickhead.

Last chance, or I'm bringing this shit to your place.

The last message was fifteen minutes ago, which means if his threat is real, he'll be here-

I don't have time to finish the thought before there's a loud bang on the door, followed by more banging.

"Jesus, Starowics, relax." When I open the door, I wince. The man looks like shit and there's something in his eyes that makes my stomach roll in fear. "What the hell happened?"

"You need to come with me. *Now.*"

"Want to tell me why?"

"Kiley," he mutters.

"What about her?"

"She's..." He rakes his fingers over his face. "She's not good."

"Where is she?"

"My place. But-" He flinches and looks away. "I wanted to take her to the hospital, but she wouldn't let me. I don't want to leave her alone for too long, 'cause I know she'll try and run again."

Fuck.

"I can't deal with this shit right now. If Brynne finds about this-"

"Kane?" Brynne is standing in the hall, holding Noah.

Shit. Shit. Shit.

"What's going on?" The familiar look of suspicion creeps back into her eyes.

"Nothing." I walk towards her, but she takes a step back.

I drag my hand through my hair and sigh.

"We need to go," Blake says behind me, desperately.

Grabbing my keys and slipping on a pair of shoes, I tell her, "I'll be back later. And I'll tell you everything. Okay?"

She doesn't look convinced. In fact, all the old mistrust

and wariness that I've worked so hard to get rid of is back and brimming with an intensity that makes my gut churn.

"This better be fucking important," I growl at Blake as I follow him toward the elevators.

He looks ready to hit me when he turns. "I don't know, asshole. Depends how much value you put on your sister's life. So far, it doesn't seem like much."

I hold my tongue as we step onto the elevator and take the five floors down to his apartment, and I steel myself for whatever it is that awaits me on the other side of the door. Nothing could have prepared me for what I find.

CHAPTER 20

rynne

HE'S HIDING SOMETHING.

Like an old friend that was never really gone, wariness creeps into the back of my mind.

Every scenario that goes through my head only makes it worse.

I didn't hear much of Kane and Blake's conversation, but the look on both their faces said, whatever they were hiding, was bad.

Maybe I'm jumping to conclusions. It's what I do. What I've always done. Especially with Kane. But I can't help but play his words over and over again in my head. *If Brynne finds out about this.*

Whatever is going on, he doesn't want me to know.

Noah whimpers in my arms, and I realize that I've been standing, staring at the closed door for over a minute. He's hungry and I'm being an idiot. Kane said he'd tell me everything when he got back, and since I've moved in with him, he's given me no reason not to trust him.

I try to ignore the cool pinpricks of premonition that tickle the back of my neck as I warm up the bottle Kane had already started making.

But as the minutes and hours pass, the initial knot in the center of my throat turns into a golf ball sized lump.

After I lay Noah down for his afternoon nap, I go to the room where Kane set up all my art supplies. Multiple finished and unfinished canvases lay scattered around.

Trust him, my heart cries out.

He's going to destroy you, my head warns.

There's a constant battle between the two.

I pull out a blank canvas and prepare my paints, then sit down to sketch the images that pop into my head. And I paint, using all my pent-up emotions to push through the self-doubt and insecurities.

I get lost in the work, only breaking when Noah wakes up from his nap.

But still, Kane isn't back. And when I check my phone, there's no message from him.

He has a practice today, which means he'll be going to the arena soon, if he's not already there.

My phone buzzes, with Felix's name popping up on the screen.

He's called twice in the past couple of days, and I haven't answered, which makes me a really shitty friend, I know.

"Hello?"

"I was starting to wonder if you were ignoring me." There's an edge of hurt to his tone, despite his attempt at humor.

"Just really busy. Trying to finish a piece for the exhibit. I can't believe how quickly-'

"About that…"

The lump in my throat drops to my stomach.

"You were supposed to have your pieces delivered to the studio two days ago. That's why I've been calling."

"Shit." I pinch the bridge of my nose. I've never been good with deadlines, but I could have sworn I had another week. "I can have a courier pick them up this afternoon-"

"They cancelled your spot, Brynne."

"What? But I can get them-"

"It's too late. I asked Lynne to hold off, but she already gave it away."

I sit down on my stool. "Can we re-book? There's another one in a few months, right?"

"I can talk to her, but..."

"But what? You know how much I wanted this. I'll do anything-"

"Why don't you come over for dinner next week? Bring Noah. And we can talk about it."

An uneasy feeling settles in my gut.

"Nothing has changed, Felix."

"So, now that you're living with Mr. Hotshot Hockey Player, you can't have dinner with a friend? Unless..." He snorts on the other end. "Unless you're already sleeping with him."

"It's not like that."

"Right," he says sarcastically.

"Felix, I-"

"Listen. I didn't want to be the one to have to tell you this, but your boyfriend isn't as golden as everyone seems to think he is."

"You don't know him."

"God, you are fucking him, aren't you?"

"That's none of your business even if I were."

"I thought you were smarter than this. But then, you did get yourself knocked up with the asshole's kid."

"I'm hanging up now."

"Fuck. I'm sorry. I didn't mean…"

"Goodbye, Felix."

"Wait." His voice is desperate.

"What?"

"Just take a look at the article I'm sending you."

"Fine," I breath out in frustration, hating what our friendship has come to.

"And Brynne. If you need me, I'm here for you."

I hang up.

A couple seconds later my phone pings with a text message. I stare at the link, not sure if I want to open it.

With a deep breath, I tap my thumb on the link and a page opens. It's some trashy online gossip magazine.

A quick glance at the article title and I know I'm going to regret opening it.

Kane Madden, Not So Golden.

I know this magazine. Ninety-nine percent of everything it reports is false, or some fabrication of the truth. But as I scroll through the bullshit and get to the incriminating photos, that damn lump returns to my throat.

The pictures are black and white and a little fuzzy, marked with a time and date stamp at the top. A quick glance and I know they were taken from the security camera just outside Kane's apartment by the parking garage entrance. They've been zoomed in, enough that Kane's features are slightly recognizable.

The first photo is of him getting out of his car. The second, him approaching a woman. She's tiny, wearing a hoodie that covers half of her face. But the half that is visible holds a look I'm all too familiar with - hollow eyes, sunken cheeks.

But it's the third picture that sends a cold shiver down my

spine. Him handing her money. Not just pocket change like he might give a homeless person, but a wad of cash.

I pace the apartment, hating the way I feel. The paranoia. The anxiety. The fear.

The logical part of my brain, even the part that's always wanted to see the worst in him, screams that there's more to the story. That there's some type of explanation. That he wasn't doing what the article said he was doing – buying drugs.

This is the shitty part about caring about someone.

Because you either have to trust them, or walk away. There's no in-between. Unless you want to drown in your own suspicions.

If this thing between Kane and I is going to work, then I have to trust him, or I should do us both a favor and end it now.

ane

"We need to take her to the ER," I growl out, frustration and concern straining every syllable.

The second I'd walked into Blake's apartment and saw a broken and beaten girl lying on his couch, my stomach had rolled. I still feel sick thinking about what kind of psychopath could hurt someone like that.

"I promised her I wouldn't." Blake leans with his back against the kitchen wall, arms crossed over his thick chest.

I place my palms on the kitchen counter, every muscle in my body tense, and let out a slow, even breath, trying to gain some semblance of patience.

"The girl is a mess. She needs-"

"The *girl* has a name." Blake's nostrils flare and he gives me a pointed look. "Maybe if you started calling her by it she'd become a person to you and not just an obligation you don't want. She's your sister, Kane."

I grunt, knowing he's right. I can't ignore the mess she's gotten herself into, not when her life is obviously at risk.

From the other room, I hear Kiley whimper. I catch a quick glance at her.

Fuck.

The girl probably weighs no more than a hundred pounds soaking wet, and her pixie-like face is all shades of blue, greens and browns. Whoever did this to her made sure not to leave an inch of her body unmarked.

"She needs an x-ray to make sure she doesn't have any broken ribs, and she's going to need at least a couple of stitches for the cut on her forehead, if not a CT scan to make sure she doesn't have a head injury."

"I already called Darryl Scallan. He's coming over-"

"You called the team's neurologist? Jesus, Blake, what's wrong with you?"

"I'm trying to help her. Which is what you should be doing. She's *your* family."

"She's a junkie. What she needs is-"

He gets in my face, grabbing my shirt and shoving me against the fridge. "Stop calling her that."

I push him away. "You're losing it, man. If this is about Sam-"

"It's not about Sam. That's your shit. It's about that girl in there. She needs help."

"Not arguing with you there." She needs ninety days in rehab and a total life make-over. But I know from experience that you can't make someone change. They have to want it. And even then, it's a long and difficult road.

"Talk to her, Kane. She's nothing like Sam. There are things you don't know. I've had a guy looking into-"

"I know she gave you some sob story, and kudos to you for caring. But she's better off in a hospital. Even if she doesn't have any serious injuries, she has to dry out. I can't have a junk-" I stop myself from saying the word when I see the fire in his eyes. Rubbing the back of my neck, I shake my head. "I'm just starting to make things work with Brynne. Christ, I've got a kid now. I can't have some girl detoxing around them."

"She can stay here."

I raise my eyebrows at him. "Here?"

"Until she gets better, and we find the asshole who did this to her."

I stare at him hard. "You're going to make her one of your charity cases, aren't you?"

"She's not a charity case. She's a person. A scared kid with nowhere else to go."

"If she really wants to get clean, I can call Cloverwood. Sam went there once. It's a nice facility."

"She's terrified, Kane. She won't go anywhere. I can get her to talk. She needs to be around people who care about her."

I narrow my eyes at him. "And you care about her?"

He takes a breath. "I care about *you*. So yeah, I do."

I hold his gaze for a long moment, then finally sigh. "This is a mistake."

He shrugs.

"Fine." I can't believe I'm agreeing to this. But what the hell else am I supposed to do?

Kiley's an adult now. So even if they admitted her, she could leave at any time. Be back on the streets in a heartbeat.

"Did she tell you what she's on?"

"I don't think she's using. At least, not lately."

I snort. "If you're going to do this, then you need to remember one thing. Always assume a junkie is using."

"She's not..." He drags his fingers through his hair and clamps his mouth shut.

"Look, I've got to get back to Brynne. She'll be wondering what's going on. And I need to deal with Coach."

I'd almost forgotten about him. I rub my palms over my eyes.

"You finally told him?"

"Brynne did, last night."

"Shit."

"Yeah."

Another small, pathetic whimper comes from the other room. Blake pushes off the wall and moves quickly toward the living room. I watch as he touches her forehead with the back of his hand, and my chest tightens when I see the emotion in his eyes.

I want to warn him not to get attached, but I have a sinking feeling in my gut he already is.

Damn it, Blake.

She might be my sister, but the man is my best friend, and I know that she can only bring one thing to his life – trouble.

She whimpers in her sleep. A gleam of sweat covers her forehead, and I wince again when I take in the bruises on her face.

Blake cleaned the dried blood off her forehead and bandaged it, but a fresh dot of red has seeped through. Lucky for her, it doesn't look like she broke anything. Anything other than her spirit.

The girl is an empty shell of a person. Broken in ways I can't even begin to imagine. Maybe if she'd come to me years ago, before she'd gotten messed up in whatever shit she's doing, I could have helped her. But she's fallen so far down the rabbit hole, I can't see how she'll be able to escape.

"You said you found her down by the parking garage?"

Blake pulls the blanket higher over her shoulder, then straightens and looks at me. "Said she was trying to get to you."

"Then why the hell didn't she come to the lobby?"

"She did." He gives me a hard stare, and I know the truth. They would have turned her away on her appearance alone.

"I'll talk with Miika at the front desk."

"Doesn't matter now. She's here. And I'm not letting her out of my sight until whoever did this to her is behind bars."

I shake my head, not understanding his possessiveness towards her, and feeling guilty that it's him and not me fighting to save her from the cursed world that's already consumed her.

But then, if it was Brynne lying there instead of Kiley, I know I'd be on the verge of murder. Difference is, Brynne would never put herself in a position where her life was in danger.

"We've got a practice in less than an hour," I say.

"I'm not leaving her."

I grunt and shake my head at him. "You're an idiot, you know that?"

He shrugs.

"Fine. I'll be back later to check on her." *And you,* I want to say.

My thoughts are a chaotic mess as I leave Blake's apartment.

"Shit," I mutter, when I glance at my phone. I won't be able to talk to Brynne if I want to make it to the practice on time. I'd think about missing it, too, but after last night's call with Coach, I need to go. I'm not looking forward to the conversation. But it has to happen.

I try calling Brynne's cell a few times on my way down to the parking garage, and again as I'm driving to the arena. But it goes straight to voicemail. On my last attempt, as I'm getting out of my car, I leave a message.

"Not sure why you're not answering your damn phone-" I swallow and try to get rid of the frustration in my voice. "I'm sorry about this morning. I'll tell you everything when I get home tonight. I..."

"Hey, loser," Sebastian smacks me on the back, making me almost drop my phone.

I glare at him, and finish my message. "We'll talk later."

"You look like shit. Hope you're not catching whatever Blake's got."

"Blake?"

"I just talked to him. He said he's got the flu or something."

"Right," I mutter, hating the lies that have piled up between us. He's going to freak out when I finally tell him about Brynne.

I'm about to say something, when I see Coach pull up in his dark green Jaguar. He slams the door when he gets out of his car, and points a finger at me. Fire blazes in his dark eyes.

"My office, Madden. After practice." I've heard that tone before, but never towards me.

When he walks away, Sebastian raises his eyebrows and whistles. "Shit. He's pissed."

"What'd you do, Madden?" Tyler Slade says, coming up behind us and slapping me a little too hard on the back. "The way Coach was glaring at you, I'd think you were screwing his daughter."

Sebastian punches him hard in the arm. "Don't be a jackass. Coach would have you traded just talking about Brynne like that."

Tyler gives me a knowing look, his lips twisting up in a viscous grin. And I know he knows.

"Yeah. I'd hate to see what he'd do to the man who actually had the balls to fuck her."

Sebastian glances between the two of us, frowning.

"See you two asshats on the rink," Tyler says, picking up

his pace, and leaving Sebastian looking like he doesn't know who to hit next, Tyler or me.

"You want to tell me something?"

I wince. "It's…"

"Jesus, Kane. Please tell me you're not that much of an idiot."

"Apparently, I am," I mutter.

Sebastian shakes his head, giving me a look of disgust. "Your funeral."

Maybe. But if Brynne is mine in the end, then whatever Coach has in store for me will be worth it.

ane

COACH SITS at his desk with my phone in his hands, flipping through the photos I'd taken of Noah.

I expect him to lose his shit at any second.

Yell.

Threaten.

Maybe even take a swing at me.

God knows, I deserve it.

But he doesn't do any of those things. He just sits there, staring at the damn phone with an odd expression on his face.

"Coach, I-"

"He looks like you."

I nod, standing there like a complete chump. "Yeah."

Silence.

"Do you love her?" He glances up at me, his gaze questioning.

"I do."

He nods, then hands me back the phone. "Good." He pulls some papers out of a folder and starts reading them, as if dismissing me.

"Coach?"

He grunts, but his attention stays on the documents in front of him.

"I...did you want..." Fuck. I don't know what I'm supposed to say. But I sound like a blabbering idiot.

"Do I want what, Madden?" His tone is sharp, and holds the first hint of anger he's shown since I came into his office after practice.

I should have kept my mouth shut, because I can almost feel the tension building inside him, ready to explode.

Ten...nine...eight...*boom*.

"You know what I would have wanted?" He stands, his face turning a deep shade of red, his voice rising with each word. "For the man I've treated like a son to have enough respect for me to tell me he knocked up my daughter. That I have a goddamn grandson. I expect this from Brynne, but you..."

He sits back down, placing the palm of his hand in the center of his chest and winces.

I take a step towards him.

He raises his hand to stop me. "I'm fine."

Sweat beads on the side of his face.

"Maybe I should call-"

"No." With some effort, he leans back in his chair, holding my gaze. "You want to do something for me, Madden? You want to make this right?"

"Yes."

"Then get me my family back."

I grimace, wishing it was that simple. "Brynne is..."

"Stubborn."

I snort. "Yeah."

"Always has been." He wipes the side of his face, his color starting to return to normal. "If I could just talk to her. Explain…" Closing his eyes, he leans his head back. "Maybe she wouldn't hate me as much."

"She doesn't hate you."

He grunts.

"I think she uses her anger as a shield not only to protect herself, but also Sam's memory."

Coach goes silent, pensive, the way he always does whenever I mention Sam.

"I always thought it was Brynne I had to worry about," he says eventually. "She looked so much like her mother." He runs his hands over his face. "And then there was her art…" His eyes gloss over and he shakes his head. "But it was Sam I should have been worried about."

I wonder if Coach had ever talked to Sam or Brynne the way he speaks to me - open, honest, like an equal - if their relationship would have been different.

"You can go," he says dismissively, resignation heavy in his voice.

I'm emotionally and physically drained when I leave the arena, and I want nothing more than to go home, wrap my arms around Brynne, and kiss her until all the shittiness of the day is forgotten. But I still have to check in on Kiley. And every mile closer I get to the apartment, I can't help but feel like there's a bomb ready to drop.

But what else could possibly go wrong today?

Kiley is awake when I come into Blake's apartment. She's sitting up on the couch, with a steaming mug in her hands. Her one good eye widens when she sees me, and I swear the girl pulls tighter into herself.

"Hey, kid," I say, sitting on the coffee table in front of her and placing my forearms on my thighs. "Looks like you're feeling better."

She nods, and glances over at Blake.

She reminds me of a bird. Fragile and nervous, ready to take flight the second she's spooked.

I realize now that I don't have to worry too much about Blake, because I doubt she'll be here come morning. Her fight or flight response is on high alert, and there's no fight left in the girl.

"Want to tell me what happened?"

"I-I told Blake. I got mugged."

Bullshit.

I sigh. "So, you don't know the person who did this to you?"

She shakes her head.

"Do you think you would recognize them if you saw them again?"

"It was dark…" Her tongue darts over her cracked bottom lip.

She's protecting someone, or she's too scared of what they'll do if she goes to the police.

"Can't help you if you don't tell us the truth."

Her fingers tremble around the mug.

"I am telling you the truth," she whispers, not meeting my gaze.

"Kiley," I say gruffly, making her flinch.

"Kane," Blake says my name behind me, and there's a warning there.

I rub my palms on my pants, then stand.

"I don't do drugs," she says softly. "I heard what you said earlier. And I wanted you to know that I don't want to hurt you or your family. I'm not…a junkie."

I can't help but grunt. "Blake said you can stay here as long as it takes for you to get back on your feet." I shove my

145

hands in my pockets and look down at her, my heart twisting in my chest for the girl staring up at me. "Once you're better, I'll look into getting you a place of your own."

She pulls her lip between her teeth again, her eyes widening. "I don't need your-"

"Yeah, you do. So, the way I see it, you have two choices. You can accept my help, or you can run. I'm not asking you to decide right now. But I will tell you this. You stay, you follow my rules."

"Rules?" Her chin is quivering now.

I'm pretty sure the kid thinks I'm an insensitive thug, or worse, but I need to make sure she knows I'm not fucking around.

"You get a job when you're able. You don't steal from me or from Blake. And absolutely no drugs."

"I don't-"

"No drugs, Kiley."

She gives a small nod. "Okay."

I watch her silently for a moment, searching for any hint of deception, but she keeps her face averted. Maybe I'm being too hard on her. But then, maybe if I'd been harder on Sam, he'd still be alive.

She fidgets with her cup, which I realize now is filled with a broth based soup that she hasn't touched.

"And, for God's sake, eat something. You look like you haven't had a meal in days."

Her gaze comes up then, and what I see guts me, because I realize how close to the truth my words are.

People talk about carrying a weight on their shoulders, but I'd never felt the actual physical presence of it until today. It's a heaviness in your very soul. A numb pain. It's an oxymoron maybe, but that's how it feels. Like the emotional pain is so heavy that your body becomes frozen from it, and you are wound so tight that at any moment you know you could snap.

That's how I feel as I push the elevator button to take me up to my apartment.

Drained.

Raw.

The only thing that keeps those pent-up emotions from spilling over is the thought of Brynne's smile this morning, the way her body trembled at my touch.

I need her tonight.

Her body.

Her heart.

Her trust.

I'm desperate for them.

The apartment is quiet and dark when I come in. I kick my shoes off, and go to her studio, but it's dark as well.

It's only quarter to ten. She never goes to sleep this early. But the lights under her bedroom door are off.

I know it's selfish waking her, but I knock anyway.

Nothing.

I open the door slightly. "Brynne?"

The bed is made, and she's not in it.

A surge of panic swells in my chest. Not really sure why, I just know something is off.

I go to Noah's room, holding my breath when I open the door, expecting to find the crib empty.

But I hear his little sucking noises, see his tiny little form spread out, the moonlight catching the shimmer of blonde hair.

I finally find Brynne sitting in the dark in the living room, staring out at the city lights, a half-empty bottle of wine on the coffee table in front of her.

"Hey. Didn't you hear me come in?"

She doesn't answer, just takes a sip of her wine.

"I'm sorry about earlier with Blake. I wanted to come back, but-"

"But what?" She looks at me then, and even in the dim light I can see the accusation in her eyes.

Every damn wall that I'd spent the past few weeks trying to tear down is back up.

"I can explain about this morning."

She laughs. "I'm sure you can. You've always been good at excuses."

"Brynne," I warn, not in the mood for a fight, my patience already hanging on by a thread.

She picks up her phone, presses something, then tosses it to me. "Unfortunately for you, pictures don't lie."

I scan the article that pops up, cursing when I see the photos of me and Kiley outside the parking garage.

The entire article is a bunch of bullshit, but then so is the website that posted it.

I don't know who I'm more upset at, the person who leaked the pictures, the person who wrote the fucking article, or the woman I love that could even for a second believe the bullshit written about me.

Anger simmers, boiling to a point where I know it's going to explode if I don't walk away.

I toss the phone back at her, then turn.

"What? Not going to defend yourself, Madden?" she says, and I can hear the couch creak as she gets up, her footsteps following me.

"Shouldn't have to."

"You promised me-"

"I promised you what?" I stop and spin towards her. She's so close she bumps into me. "Tell me, Brynne. What do you think I did? What promise did I break?" My voice goes icy, a tone I've never really used with her. "I want you to think real hard before you accuse me."

She sways a little, reminding me that she's been drinking. But it's not an excuse.

"Who is she? Your dealer? An ex? You gave her money. You can't deny that."

I hold her gaze, seeing every accusation she doesn't say.

"Yeah, Brynne. She's my fucking drug dealer." Sarcasm and bitterness drip from my words, but despite that, I can tell she believes me.

Hurt twists in my chest. And I know she'll never really trust me. No matter what I do, I'll always be the guy who killed her brother.

"Enough." I take a step towards her, but she holds her ground, jutting her chin up at me. "No more, Brynne. I'm sick of this. Sick of you always thinking the worst of me. I can deal with a lot of shit. But not this. Not from you, and not tonight."

"Don't act like you're the victim here-"

"Is that what you think you are? A victim?" I snort and drag my hands over my face.

"I didn't say that. But I'm not the one with pictures all over the internet looking like you're making some sort of-"

"You want to know who she is?" I yell, making her wince.

"I want the truth."

"Bullshit. You want something you can use against me so that you don't have to feel the things you do." I stalk towards her, and she backs up until she's flat against the wall, and I shoot my arms out, palms flat beside her. I lean down, narrowing my eyes at her, my breathing rough, my emotions frayed. "You keep pushing me away. Wanting me to fuck up. Because you're too damn scared to admit you care about me."

She doesn't respond, just holds my gaze.

"You think you're strong. Think that steel cage you've got yourself trapped in is going to protect you from getting hurt. But it just makes you a *coward*."

She sucks in a breath, and I know I've hit a nerve. And like the asshole I feel I am right now, I push at it harder.

"Admit it, Brynne. You're a coward. You've got everything you want standing right in front of you, but you're too damn scared to take it."

Her bottom lip trembles, and for a second I think she's going to break. To finally admit the truth. But instead, I see her expression cloud over, and the stubborn set of her jaw returns.

"You're trying to change the subject."

I let out a bitter laugh. "No, sweetheart. I'm just trying to make you see the truth. I've been too worried about protecting you, but it's obvious you don't need or want my protection."

"You're right. I don't."

I hold her gaze, but there's no give there, just wall after wall of self-preservation.

God, I love her so damn much it hurts. But right now, I wonder if it wouldn't hurt less to walk away.

I push off the wall and take a step back.

"The girl in the pictures is my sister." There's no emotion in my voice, just cold, hard resignation.

"You don't have a sister."

"I do. But you'd know that if you hadn't hidden from me like a fucking coward for the past year."

Her mouth parts, eyes widening slightly. Maybe she believes me. Maybe she doesn't. Normally, I'd care. But right now, anger is the only thing that consumes me.

"You think you're the only one in this world who deals with shit? We all have our problems, and we face them. You don't run away like some scared teenager. Your brother died. He killed himself. Yeah, it sucks. But stop taking it out on everyone who loves you. Or you know what? You're going to push everyone away, and you'll have no one. Not even me."

She sucks in a shaky breath, her eyes wide. "Kane-"

"Save it." I rub the back of my neck where all the tension sits like a heavy stone. "I've had a long, shitty day. Funny thing is, I couldn't wait to come home to see you. But I should have figured you'd find something to sabotage what we have." I walk away, but toss one last truth over my shoulder. "You always do."

rynne

KANE STORMS TOWARDS HIS BEDROOM, and even though I want nothing more than to follow him, I don't move.

Can't.

I wince as the door slams behind him.

Every one of his harsh words burns through me. I've allowed my fears and insecurities to destroy the trust he's been so careful to build between us.

This whole time, it's been him who's tried to make this work.

"You're an idiot," I mumble to myself, picking up my phone and deleting the link Felix sent me.

I was upset about my exhibit being cancelled. Angry at Felix. But once again, I directed that frustration towards Kane.

Fix it. I shake my head. I've never been good at apologies. But I know I owe him one.

I knock on his bedroom door and wait, but there's no answer.

That scared, insecure little girl inside me demands that I walk away. But if I do, I may never have the courage to say what's eating at me.

"Kane." I try the handle. It's unlocked. I open the door, but he's not in bed.

I can hear the shower in his bathroom.

The thought of Kane wet and naked does all sorts of things to my body. Sex would be an easy way out. A way to apologize without having to say the damn words.

"Coward," I mutter. And I am. I've always been with him.

Pulling my bottom lip between my teeth, I bite hard, and take a deep breath before walking into the large bathroom. That same breath gets stuck in my throat when I see him behind the glass wall, his muscles bunching and rippling with every small movement.

Water cascades down his sculpted back, and his dark hair is plastered against his forehead. Both palms are pressed against the wall in front of him, and I can hear him muttering something incoherent through the hiss of water.

His eyes are closed, his features pulled tight in frustration. He slams his fist against the tiles.

I jump slightly. Maybe this wasn't a good idea.

But just when I'm about to make my escape, his eyes open, his gaze latching on to mine.

Frozen. Like an animal trapped in a predator's gaze. That's how I feel as he slowly turns off the water and opens the glass door.

He grabs a towel and wraps it around his waist, his hard, blue eyes never leaving mine.

"Well?" He raises a dark eyebrow at me. "You come to accuse me of something else?"

"No." I swallow, unable to resist dragging my gaze down

his torso, watching how the small droplets of water slide across his smooth skin.

"Brynne?" He growls my name.

"Yeah?" I jerk my eyes back to his.

He's smirking now. But there's nothing nice about it. Just a knowing twitch of his lips. He takes a step towards me and his towel slides free. He does nothing to stop it from falling, nothing to hide the growing erection between his legs.

"Is this what you came in here for?" His words are clipped despite the hunger beneath them.

"No." I shake my head, but the word sounds more like a whimper.

He sneers and takes another step toward me. "You sure?"

"I don't want to fight with you."

"Could've fooled me." Another step, and he's a breath away.

My fingers curl into fists beside me, resisting the temptation to touch him.

"You're going to drive me insane, you know that?" He reaches out and drags his knuckles across my cheek.

I tremble and close my eyes.

His touch. It's the purest thing in the world. But my heart is so corrupted that I haven't been able to see it.

"I'm sorry," I whisper. "You're right."

He stills.

I open my eyes and find him staring at me.

One eye twitches, before he asks, "About what?"

"Everything."

"You're going to have to be a bit more specific, sweetheart, if you're wanting to make this a real apology."

"You're not going to make this easy on me, are you?"

He exhales through his nose, lips tightening, his hand cupping the back of my neck, fingers tangling in my hair, and growls out one word. "No."

I sigh. "I haven't been fair to you."

He grunts.

"And you're right. I do…care."

A small smile tugs at his lips, but there's that damn sadness still lingering in his eyes. "Wish that was enough."

"It's all I have right now."

"Bullshit." He untangles his fingers and drops his hand to his side. "It's all you're willing to give."

"Maybe."

He shakes his head and crosses his arms. "I want more."

"I know."

I'm not a touchy person. Never have been. And I'm definitely not a mushy one. But right now, my heart feels all sorts of things I know I shouldn't.

Or maybe it should.

I've been fighting him so damn long, and all it's brought is heartache.

"What do you want?" I ask.

His nostrils flare. "Your trust."

I give a small nod. "Okay."

He gives me a skeptical look.

"What else?"

"Let's just start with that for now."

A part of me sags because I want him to ask for more. I want him to demand it. It may be the only way I can give it to him.

He moves past me, walking back into the bedroom, and pulls out a pair of jogging pants from a drawer and puts them on.

I watch him. Every movement. He's so familiar to me, and yet there's still this huge gulf between us.

"Do you want to tell me about her?"

He looks at me, rubs the back of his neck and shrugs. "Her name's Kiley. She's my half-sister. Was born when I was put into foster care, so I didn't know about her. She showed up less than a year ago. Didn't believe her at first. By the time I realized she was telling the truth, she'd taken off."

"But she's back now?"

"Staying with Blake. She got into some…trouble."

"What kind of trouble?"

"Trouble I didn't want you having to deal with…again."

"Oh." I sit down on the edge of the bed. "Why didn't you tell me about her?"

He exhales heavily. "Because I don't know what kind of shit she's messed up in. And I don't want her around you and Noah. Especially not after everything with…"

"Sam."

"Yeah."

"Trying to protect me," I mutter.

"Always," is his muffled reply.

My heart pounds in my chest, aching with an emotion I don't want to name.

I stand and walk towards him, reaching up and placing my palms on his chest.

He doesn't move. Just watches me.

"No more," I say, standing on tiptoes and brushing my mouth against his.

"No more what?" He still doesn't touch me. Our lust is thick and heavy between us. But it's so much more than that. It's a connection I've been too scared to admit.

"No more protecting me." I press against him, feeling his cock strain against his pants.

"Can't help it. Made a promise." His words are strained as I kiss his jaw, his neck, his collarbone.

"If we're going to do this, then I need to know you're being honest with me. That you're not keeping things from me, even if it's for my protection."

He sighs. "I won't lie to you, Brynne."

My fingers skim over his chest, down each sculpted ab.

He captures my wrists. "But I will *always* protect you. Always, Brynne."

I try to swallow, but it feels like there's something lodged in my throat.

"I…" *Love you.*

Damn. Why are those three words so hard to say?

His lips twitch up slightly, and he places my hands around his neck. "You what?"

I love you and it scares me more than anything ever has.

Pressing against him, I whisper against his lips. "I want to finish what we started this morning."

He runs his hands down my back, his heavy erection against my stomach. "And I want you in my bed. *Every night.* That's my condition."

I raise my eyebrows at him. "Already making demands?"

He nips at my bottom lip, then scoops me up. "Yes."

A heartbeat later, my back is pressed firmly against the mattress and his hulking form hovers above me.

Everything between us has always been tense, volatile, but there's none of that in his eyes right now. What I see makes my chest ache.

Acceptance. That's one thing he's always given me.

Love. I've tried so hard to deny it, but it's there, blazing in the blue depths.

But it's the possessiveness, an almost primal look of ownership that makes me tremble.

"I-"

"No more talking," he growls out, crushing his lips against mine.

His kiss is wild. *Feral.*

He moves between my legs, his hips pressed against mine, and I wiggle beneath him, moaning with the friction against my already pulsing clit.

I want this.

Him.

Always have.

Slowly, he undresses me. His fingers are hard, callused, and deliciously rough against my sensitive skin.

"So beautiful," he murmurs, taking his time, kissing every inch of my body.

I half expect, half hope for him to take me hard and fast. With all the tension that has simmered between us for so long, I wouldn't have blamed him. What I don't expect is the way he watches me, as his fingers, his mouth, his tongue dance across my skin.

My hips arch upwards as he slips a finger inside me and his tongue licks across my folds.

"Kane," I say softly, breathlessly.

His mouth devours me. He sucks and licks at my swollen clit until I'm moaning for more. For all of him.

I plunge my fingers into his still damp hair, and pull slightly. "Kane, please."

Blue eyes meet mine, and he grins, before giving one last lick that makes my entire body quiver.

"Please, what?" He crawls up my body, wedging himself between my thighs. "What do you want, Brynne?"

He's going to make me say it.

"You," I admit.

His lips twitch up, and he places his palms beside my shoulders, holding himself above me, the swollen crest of his cock teasing my entrance.

I grip his hips, my nails digging into his skin as I wiggle beneath him.

"Then you accept my terms?" He lifts an eyebrow.

He wants me here. In his bed. Every night.

I want it, too.

"Yes."

His mouth is back on mine. And I feel some of that steel-like self-control of his slipping.

"Good," he groans against my lips.

I wrap my legs around his waist and angle my hips, begging with my body to feel him fill me.

"Are you on the pill?" he asks.

I can't help but chuckle.

"What?" He arches a dark brow.

"Probably something we should have thought about last time."

He nips at my bottom lip. "Last time, I wasn't thinking."

"And you are now?" It's meant to be a tease, but his expression is serious.

"I'm thinking about a lot of things."

I tremble, but this time not from his touch. From the promises and expectations in his eyes. And I see it - our future.

"I'm on the pill," I say breathlessly.

He doesn't hesitate. He thrusts into me with one hard move and I cry out, taking every inch of him, his thick cock stretching and filling me completely.

And I know there's no denying that he owns every piece of me.

My heart.

My mind.

My tattered soul.

It's all his.

He lets out a long breath, holding himself above me, before he starts to move.

"I love you," he growls against my mouth, between kissing me. "So damn much."

I moan and my head falls back, eyes closed, taking in every feeling, every emotion, like it's the first time.

"Kane," I pant his name, each delicious thrust sending me closer to the edge.

He consumes me, the inferno between us building.

"Come with me, Brynne," he growls out, holding my gaze.

I can't hold back. My body trembles and shakes. White flashes of light blind my vision, and I cry out his name, digging my nails into his shoulders as I ride every wave of pleasure.

He drives into me one last time, burying himself to the hilt as he spills himself inside of me.

I keep my legs wrapped around him, holding him there.

Our bodies are damp with sweat. He's heavy, but I love his weight on top of me. I run my fingers over his stomach, watching the muscles ripple under my touch.

We lay in silence, and heavy breaths are the only sound between us.

"You're everything," he mumbles against my hair.

I trace the dark patterns of the tattoos on his arm.

I love you, my heart beats, begging me to say those three simple words. To give him the confirmation that I'm his.

But he already knows it. And I'm grateful he doesn't demand the words.

"I talked with Coach today," he says, his voice heavy with sleep.

"And?" I twist in his arms, so that my chin is on his chest. "Are we going to be apartment shopping in Toronto?"

He chuckles. "I don't think he hates me that much."

"I'm sorry you had to deal with him alone. I shouldn't have…"

"Two apologies in one night. That must be a record." He quirks an eyebrow at me.

I slap his chest lightly. "And you'll never hear another one from me again if you make a big deal about it."

"Fair enough." He tucks my hair behind my ear. "Actually, he wasn't as upset as I thought he'd be. He was hurt, but-"

"Hurt? What right does he have-" I try to move away, but he pins me with his heavy arm.

"He's your father. And you didn't tell him you had a kid."

"You're defending him?"

"I'm just saying I can understand how he feels."

I grunt, wiggling to get away, but he doesn't let me.

"My bed." He presses his lips against my forehead. "You promised. Be pissed at me, but don't run away."

I relax slightly, although I'm still frustrated that he would take my father's side.

"He loves you, Brynne."

I shrug. "He loves you more. You and that damn team. Always has."

"You're wrong."

"I'm not."

He growls against my ear. "Do you always have to have the last word?"

"Yes." I smile up at him, grinning.

He sighs, holding me tighter. "You're a pain in the ass, you know that?"

"Yeah, but you love me." The words are out of my mouth before I even realize what I'm saying.

His gaze narrows, his expression hard and serious. "Yeah. I do."

I swallow hard. "Kane…"

I love you, too.

The words stick in my throat.

"I…"

"One day." He presses his lips against my forehead. "I'm going to ask you to marry me."

"Kane-"

"Don't worry, sweetheart. It's not tonight. I won't ask you

again until I know you're ready. But one day you will say yes."

I don't respond, because if I do, I know I'll probably beg him to ask me now.

But he's right. I'm not ready. I don't know if I'll ever be.

I never wanted any of this.

The thought of marriage. Kids. Playing house. It was never my dream. My dream was to paint. To create. To be my own person. Not to be a hockey wife. And with Kane, that's what I'll be.

CHAPTER 24

 ane

BRYNNE MUMBLES IN HER SLEEP, one arm strung possessively over my chest, a leg looped around mine.

It's still dark outside, but I can already hear Noah starting to stir through the monitor.

I hate getting out of bed, hate leaving her, but we were up half the night, and I want to let her sleep. Carefully, I shift out of bed, then pull the covers over her shoulders.

After I change and feed Noah, I wrap him in a blanket, take him out on the balcony, and watch the sun rise over the city.

"One step closer, buddy. She still won't admit that she loves me. But she does."

Noah babbles his response and I grin down at him.

Never thought I wanted to be a dad. But him. He's perfect. My heart swells with pride, and I want nothing more than to tell everyone he's mine.

I'm done with the pretenses.

"And we're going to have to do something about that damn birth certificate," I mutter. "Because you will have my name. You're a Madden."

"Ma, ma, ma," he jabbers.

"Close," I chuckle, then say slowly. "Ma-dden."

"Da, da, da."

I chuckle. "Yeah, I'm your daddy."

I wonder if all babies are as smart as him. I doubt it. But I could just be suffering from what Blake calls Daddy-fever, the belief that everything your kid does is a world event that deserves media coverage.

We used to laugh at the guys who came in with their videos and pictures, but I get it now. I don't want to miss a moment with him. And if I could record every second of his precious life, I would.

"Hi," Brynne says, closing the balcony door behind her as she steps out. She's wearing one of my oversized t-shirts, her face clean of make-up, her dark hair tangled, and I swear she's never looked more beautiful.

"You two look content." She smiles, reaching for Noah's hand when he starts to gurgle at her.

I place my palm on her cheek and lean down, brushing my lips across hers, and I feel her tremble.

"Come inside and I'll make you coffee."

She nods, following me.

I place Noah in his chair, then pour us both a coffee.

She shifts nervously under my gaze, taking a sip.

"It's time we told people." I lean against the counter, catching her gaze roam across my body as it always does when she thinks I'm not looking.

"My father knows. It's no one else's business."

I ignore the simmering frustration that stirs in my chest.

"Thought you and Noah could come to the game tonight. There's a box for the wives-"

"I'm not your wife."

"Not yet."

"Kane-"

"I know." I sigh, placing my cup in the sink, then removing the distance between us.

"This is a lot all at once," she says when I wrap my arms around her waist, her palms coming up to my chest. "I just think we should take things slow."

I place my forehead against hers and mutter, "Stubborn."

She shrugs, slipping her hands under my shirt, and giving me a teasing grin. "You already got me in your bed. What else do you want, Madden?"

"Everything, sweetheart. I want everything." I kiss her, feeling her body melt against me. "And I have every intention of getting it, because I have something that trumps stubbornness."

"What's that?" she asks, slightly breathless.

"Perseverance."

CHAPTER 25

rynne

STUBBORN.

That's what he called me.

I know he's right. Especially with him. But old habits die hard. And even though my heart is begging me to take the leap of faith, I can't help but think I'm going to lose myself if I do.

"You're already living with him," I mumble as I put the finishing touches on a painting I've been working on. "What difference does it really make if people know?"

All the difference.

Because the second the world knows, the harder it will be to run.

My gut does a somersault as the thought goes through my head.

I don't want to run. Not anymore. Not from Kane.

But his life, the world he lives in—I've spent years trying

to get away from it. Hating it. Blaming it for Sam's death. For the childhood I missed out on.

I know that Kane isn't my father. But there's still that nagging feeling in the back of my head that is scared of jumping in with both feet.

Maybe you should have thought about that before you slept with him, my brain chastises.

But sex and marriage are very different things.

Sex, you can walk away from.

"Who am I kidding?" I toss my dirty brushes in the sink. I'll never walk away from him. Never again. Not without losing a piece of myself.

I'm in deep. Deeper than I ever thought possible.

There's a bang on the door.

I'd ignore it, except Noah just went down for his nap, and I'm afraid if the person keeps knocking, they'll wake him up.

"Oh," the girl says with a frown when I open the door. Dark hair hangs over her face, but it doesn't hide the bruises, the black eye that is swollen shut, or the deep purple bruise on her jaw. "I…Sorry. I must have the wrong apartment."

I know who she is immediately, from the photos Felix sent me.

"You're Kiley, right?"

Her eyes widen and she nods.

"I'm Brynne. I'm Kane's…" God, what am I? It feels weird calling myself his girlfriend, so I just say, "Why don't you come in."

"I don't know." She shifts nervously, glancing over her shoulder at the elevator.

Noah's cry echoes down the hall, and I curse inwardly. His afternoon naps are getting shorter and shorter lately.

Kiley's eyes widen at the sound. "You have a baby?"

"I do."

"Is…is it Kane's?"

"Yeah." Which makes him her nephew. It's an odd thought, one I hadn't considered before.

We stand there in awkward silence for another few seconds. But Noah's cries keep getting louder.

"I need to get him."

She nods, then starts to turn.

I hesitate, then say, "Would you like to meet him?"

"I..." She frowns, but when I open the door wider she steps in, and I get a real sense of how tiny she is. She's got on a baggy hoodie, but it doesn't hide the fact that she's severely underweight. "Okay."

"You're staying with Blake, right?" I say, leading her into the living room.

She lifts her shoulders, not responding. There's pain written all over the girl. Pain and heartache. And I know why Kane didn't want me to meet her. She reminds me of Sam, with the same lost, desperate look.

I reach down into the playpen and lift Noah out. He hiccups a couple times before finally settling down.

Her expression softens when she sees him. "I didn't know Kane had a kid."

"It's been complicated. We haven't told many people."

She frowns. "I don't think Kane would want me here."

I know she's right. But the girl in front of me isn't a threat. She just needs help.

"Do you want to hold him?" I ask.

She shakes her head and looks over her shoulder, like she expects Kane to come storming through the doors.

"I shouldn't. I just came here to give him this." She pulls a folding letter out of her pocket and hands it to me.

I know the look in her eyes. It's one I can relate to - *fear*. Whatever the letter says, I know what she's planning - she's going to run. And if she does, she'll be running straight back into the trouble she just got out of.

"Why don't you stay for a bit?" When she starts to protest, I don't give her the chance to walk away. I place Noah in her arms, and start towards the kitchen. "I was just about to start preparing dinner, and I'd really appreciate the company. Plus, you can help keep Noah entertained. He gets a bit fussy at this time if he's not being held."

"I don't think-"

"You'd be doing me a favor."

She looks down at Noah, shifting him in her arms, and mumbles, "Okay."

"Good. Do you like spaghetti and meatballs?"

She nods.

From the kitchen, I watch her interact with Noah as I start dicing the garlic. When the sauce is simmering on the oven, I sit down on the couch opposite them.

"You're good with him."

She shrugs. "I'm used to being around babies."

I remember Kane saying something about the foster families she'd been in, but I don't press her.

Silence stretches between us, and I can see pink creep into her cheeks as I study her.

"I know what you think of me," she says, bouncing Noah on her lap.

"What's that?"

"Same thing Kane does. That I'm here for his money."

"Are you?"

"No."

"Okay."

"And I'm not a charity case, either. I can take care of myself."

"I'm sure you can. But it looks like right now you could use a little help."

She winces. "Help always comes with conditions."

I pick up the letter from the coffee table that she'd given me earlier, and turn it over in my fingers.

"You're right. People never do things without a reason."

"Yeah." She gives me a skeptical look.

"But sometimes that reason is that they care about you."

"If you're talking about Kane, then you're wrong. When I found out I had a brother, even before I knew who he was, I thought maybe…" She touches Noah's cheek. "Maybe I could finally have a family."

"You can, Kiley. You do."

"No." She stands, wincing as she does, then places Noah back in his playpen. "Kane hates me. I don't know why. But I see it in his eyes. He doesn't want me here. Not that I blame him. He's got this whole perfect life. And I'm just a reminder of where he comes from."

"You're wrong."

"Am I?" She's shaking as she stands there, a small hint of fire burning in her eyes, which gives me a small ounce of hope that she still has something left inside of her to fight.

"I think you scare him." I stand and take a step towards her. "In a way, you scare me, too."

Hurt fills her expression. "I'm not a thief, if that's what you're worried about."

"No. God, no. That's not what I meant."

"Then what? Are you convinced I'm a junkie, too? I know that's what Kane thinks. But I'm not."

I suck in a shaky breath, and tell her the truth. "We lost someone a couple years ago. Someone we both cared a lot about. You remind me of him."

Silence.

She fidgets, shifting her weight from one foot to the other. "I'm sorry about your friend, but-"

"He was my brother." I swallow hard. "He overdosed two

years ago. Both Kane and I tried to help him…but he wouldn't let us."

She shivers and looks down at the floor.

"So, yeah. You scare me." I take her hand, careful not to squeeze too hard when I see the bruises there. "But you're Kane's family. Which means your mine and Noah's, too."

Her eyes shut, she inhales through her nose, and I can tell she's trying to hold back tears.

"You know what I think?" I say softly.

"What?"

"I think you're a lot like me."

Her eyes widen. "No."

"Yeah. You are. You're strong. Stronger than you think. But you push people away because you know that feeling anything more than indifference is dangerous. Someone hurt you. And not just the bruises on your body."

"You don't know me."

"You're right. But I want to."

Her fingers are ice cold in mine, and they tremble the way Sam's used to, but I'm starting to wonder if it's not for a different reason.

"Come back and sit down. I'll finish making dinner and then we can watch the game together."

"I'm not a junkie," she whispers again, sucking in a breath and glancing away. "I just…there are things…"

"You're shaking." I place an arm carefully around her shoulder and lead her back to the living room. "How long has it been? Since you used?"

Her cheeks stain red. "I haven't-"

"Kiley." I give her a stern look.

"A couple weeks. But it was only pot. I swear."

I nod, trying to keep all judgement from my expression. Not sure if I believe her. But I don't know her story. And part of me wonders if I want to. The girl is damaged in ways that most people would never recover from.

But I was telling her the truth when I said she's family. And even if it means facing Kane's wrath, I won't let the girl run away. Not without a fight.

Like Kane says, I'm stubborn. And she's not the first Madden I've come up against.

CHAPTER 26

ane

ONE MORE WIN under our belts and we've guaranteed a playoff position. It feels good. But not as good as going home and knowing Brynne is waiting there for me.

She's at the door when I walk in the apartment.

Tossing my stuff on the floor, I pull her against me and kiss her hard. "I could get used to this."

"What?" She asks breathlessly, her body melting against mine.

"You waiting up for me." I kiss her again, then nip at her bottom lip. "But it's late. You should be in bed. Naked." I nuzzle my nose against her ear and inhale her scent. "Very, very, naked."

She laughs, but her palms come up to my chest and she pushes back. "I have to tell you something."

I groan, because the last thing I want to do right now is talk.

"Can it wait?" I kiss her jaw, her neck. "Because I'm really enjoying this, and I have a feeling whatever you're about to say is going to put a damper on what I want to do to you."

"Kane."

"All right." I sigh, straightening, but not releasing her. "What is it?"

"Don't be mad, okay?"

I grunt. "That doesn't sound good."

"I just wanted you to know before you go into-"

A harsh knock on the door makes Brynne jump.

I frown and look down at her. "Expecting someone?"

She shakes her head.

More banging.

Shit.

I go to the door, frowning when I open it and see Blake there, the look on his face tortured and frantic.

"What's wrong?"

"She's gone." He leans against the doorframe, breathing hard. "Kiley. She's not at my apartment. Her things are still there. But she's-"

"She's here," Brynne says, coming up behind me and placing her hand on my arm. "She came up looking for Kane, and I asked her to stay for dinner. She fell asleep while we were watching the game and I didn't want to disturb her."

Blake's shoulders sag and he lets out a low breath.

All the tension that I released on the ice tonight returns. "She's here?"

Brynne nods, chewing on her bottom lip like she's been caught doing something she knew I'd be upset about. And she's right. I'm furious she'd let the girl in without talking to me. God only knows what could have happened.

"She's sleeping on the couch. That's what I wanted to tell you."

I hold her gaze, my jaw tightening. "Brynne-"

"We talked for a long time. It was nice-"

"Brynne," I say again, but she keeps chattering on like the words will somehow stop the frustration building within me.

Blake looks between us, his brows drawn down.

"...and she spent some time with Noah."

"You let her around Noah?" I drag my fingers through my hair, ignoring the glare Blake sends me. "You should have talked to me before bringing her in here."

Brynne frowns. "She's your sister."

"She's a-"

"Kane." The word is a warning from Blake, and when I follow his gaze, I meet Kiley's waif-like eyes.

"I knew this was a bad idea," she mumbles, keeping her head down as she walks to the door. "I'll go." She gives Brynne a weak smile. "Thank you for dinner."

Blake is glaring daggers at me, and Brynne pinches my arm hard, but I let the girl leave, shutting the door hard behind them.

Brynne's arms are crossed when I turn back to her.

"What was that?"

I shake my head at her. "You shouldn't have let her in."

"Why, because she's struggling? She's not dangerous, she just needs help."

"And I'll help her. But..." My neck is tense, the muscles cramping, and I rub my palm over them.

Brynne says softly, "She's not Sam."

I frown at her. It's the same thing Blake said. "I know that."

"I talked to her. And I don't think drugs are the problem."

"Bullshit. You saw her. She's an addict."

"She's scared. I don't know what of. But I don't think she's an-"

"Maybe she's a better liar than I gave her credit for."

"What's your problem with her?"

175

"My problem is she came here looking for a handout because she's too stoned to work in order to support her habit." Irrational anger mixed with fear rises up in my throat.

Fear of Brynne getting attached, of her getting hurt again. Of what the girl could bring into our lives. But more specifically, fear of losing another person I care about to drugs.

Brynne steps towards me and places her palms on my chest. "I'm sorry."

"For what?" I spit out.

"For not seeing how much pain you were in. For thinking Sam's death only affected me. I was selfish. But you can't turn your back on her because you're afraid she'll end up like him."

I rest my forehead against hers and sigh. "Maybe you're right."

"I usually am," she smiles up at me.

I grunt, wrapping my arms around her. "You're also sexy as hell."

Her lips quirk up. "Now that we're alone, I can think of some things I'd rather do than argue."

"Really?" I raise an eyebrow. "Like what?"

Her fingers move to my belt, unfastening it, and I groan when I hear the snap of my jeans button, the zip of the zipper.

"Like tasting you." She licks her lips, and I lose all fucking control.

I don't care that we're in the middle of the hallway. I tug at her shirt, as her own hands desperately attack my clothes.

"God, Brynne," I groan, when she drops to her knees and takes my cock into her warm, wet mouth.

Her tongue lashes out at the head of my cock. I twist my fingers in her hair and watch as she takes me deep, then pulls back, glancing up at me with a wicked little smile.

My cell rings somewhere in the pile of discarded clothes.

I ignore it, but when it rings for the third time, Brynne releases me and stands, raking her nails down my chest.

"Should you get it?"

"No fucking way," I growl, crashing my lips against hers, wanting to find the damn phone and toss it off the balcony.

It rings again.

Brynne mumbles against my lips, "Maybe you should-"

"Shit," I mutter. The universe is not on my side tonight. I rummage through the clothes and find my phone, answering gruffly, "Yeah?"

"Mr. Madden?"

"Speaking."

"I'm calling from University Hospital. I have you listed as a contact for Steven Jacobs."

I glance over at Brynne, who's watching me with raised eyebrows, and my throat sinks into my chest. She must see it, because concern flashes in her eyes.

"Is he all right?" I ask, already knowing the answer. They wouldn't have called if he was.

"He was brought in by ambulance. He has had a heart attack. I suggest that you get here as soon as you can."

 rynne

I'm numb as I sit in the small waiting area that slowly fills with players and some of their wives. We've been here for hours, and all I know at this point is that my father had a heart attack and he's in surgery.

It's late, or early, depending how you look at it, but as exhausted as I am, I can't close my eyes. All I can think is that this is my fault.

Rationally, I know it isn't. But the guilt is still there.

And then there's the way the players and their wives keep looking at me. Most don't make it obvious, but I keep catching their glances, and the way they quickly look away.

Kane crouches in front of me, holding Noah, who's fast asleep in his arms. "Are you sure you don't want to go lie down? There's a room-"

"I'm fine."

He nods and places a hand on my knee, which causes more raised brows.

"Why are they all here?" I say with more frustration than I have a right to feel. But I can't help it as I glance around the room, feeling the weight of their stares.

Kane watches me with the same concern in his eyes he's had since he received the phone call.

He received the call. That's another thing that pricks at my chest. That Kane, rather than his own daughter, was his emergency contact.

"Do you want me to ask them to leave?"

"No." What right do I have to do that? If anything, they have more right to be here than I do. They're my father's real family. I'm just the prodigal daughter – or, at least, that's what I see in their eyes.

Judgement.

Suspicion.

And maybe I deserve some of it. I can imagine what my relationship with my father must look like to them. They worship the man. And, in a way, I don't blame them. Because I once did, too.

There was no one like my dad. He was the biggest and strongest man I knew. And I saw the way people looked at him. With awe and reverence. Like he was their hero. Even now, I can see it in the players' eyes.

The man was like a god. Strong. Indestructible. Unbreakable. It was easy to think that nothing would ever happen to him. That I had all the time in the world to be angry at him. To work out my frustrations – alone.

But if he dies...

I swallow hard, blinking back the tears that burn my eyes.

There are still so many things left unresolved between us. So much that still needs to be forgiven. Between both of us.

It took tonight for me to realize that I need his forgiveness just as much as he needs mine.

But now, I may never get it.

"He's going to be all right," Kane says, squeezing my hand, his words brimming with the confidence I don't feel. He stands when Noah starts to fuss, then picks up the diaper bag. "I'm going to see if I can find somewhere to heat up a bottle."

I watch him walk out of the room carrying our son. It's odd to see him with Noah in front of all these people, and I wonder how many of them have figured out that Noah is his.

Other than Blake, who isn't here, I'm not sure who else Kane has told.

"I thought you could use a coffee." One of the wives sits down beside me and hands me a Styrofoam cup filled with tarry looking liquid. "It came out of one of those machines, so I'm not sure how good it will be."

"Thank you," I say, taking it, and trying not to grimace when I take a sip.

"I'm Sophie." She gives me a small, concerned smile.

"Brynne."

She nods. "I know. Your father showed me your pictures."

I frown at her. "He did?"

"And some of your art as well. You're very talented."

"Thanks," I mutter, not sure how to handle the confession. It doesn't seem like something he would do.

"How are you holding up?" she asks, her deep brown eyes filled with genuine concern.

"I just wish they'd tell us something."

"Waiting is always the hardest."

No. Death is, I want to say. But I just nod.

We sit in silence for a few minutes, but when Kane comes back into the room and sits in one of the far chairs holding Noah, feeding him his bottle, the whispering begins again.

"He's yours?" she asks, nodding at Noah.

"Yes." Immediately, my walls go up, waiting for the probing to start.

"I have three," she says, her eyes filling with pride. "Lily is eight. Emma is five. And the baby, Thomas, is two." She pulls out her phone to show me pictures. "They grow up so fast. But the first couple years, I wondered if I'd ever sleep again. I had Matt, but you know their schedule. Some days, I feel like a single parent."

She's not prying, but I can see all the questions in her eyes. The same questions that everyone wants to ask, but hasn't. They just keep tiptoeing around me. Whispering.

"He's Kane's. If that's what you're wondering."

Her eyes widen slightly, but I give her credit, because there's no judgment there, just normal curiosity.

"He looks like him."

"He does." I'm sure everyone else in the room is thinking the same thing.

I doubt this is the way Kane wanted to tell people, but it's out now. And, in a way, it's like a weight has been lifted from my shoulders. No more secrets.

"Are you two together?" she asks. Normally, I'd tell the woman to mind her own business, but I can tell that she's interested not for the sake of gossip, but because she cares for Kane.

That's one thing the Annihilators have always encouraged - a sense of family among the players. If only my father would have brought that same sense of responsibility home with him.

Kane looks over at me, as if he heard Sophie's question, which I know he couldn't, not with people talking around us. But he raises an eyebrow as if in expectation of an answer.

"Yeah." I pull my bottom lip between my teeth and nod.

"Good." She smiles, then squeezes my hand. "He's one of the good ones. But then, I guess you already know that."

I look at Kane, who's still watching me while holding a conversation with a couple of the other players. Noah reaches out to grab at the dark scruff on his jaw. Kane pulls his tiny fist away, kissing it before saying something to him that makes him give a full out baby-laugh around the bottle.

Kane laughs with him, and I see the brows around the room raise again.

When Sophie gets up to leave, a dark-haired man with piercing green eyes, that I recognize as Sebastian Wilde, takes her seat. He stretches his long legs out in front of him, rubbing his palms over his jeans.

I've known the man almost as long as I've known Kane. But he was never friends with Sam, so except for team parties, or the occasional game that I went to, I didn't speak to him much. He was always just another arrogant hockey player who thought too highly of himself and made way too much money at far too young of an age.

He sits in silence. Even though I can tell he wants to say something, he just keeps staring at Kane with a worried expression on his face.

"Kane told you?" I ask, knowing Sebastian is one of his close friends. "About us."

He gives me a side glance, and I see the flicker of suspicion and hurt in his gaze. "No."

"Oh."

"Figured it out tonight, though. The kid's his?"

I nod, and he grunts in response.

"I know you two have some fucked up history together," he says, his voice low enough that only I can hear. "But you hurt him…"

There's a look of warning in his eyes.

"You don't have to worry about Kane. He can take care of himself."

Sebastian grunts. "He's been a mess for the past year. Didn't know why. Now I do."

He holds my gaze.

"Everything okay?" Kane is hovering above us, his brows drawn down. I didn't even see him get up.

"Yeah." I stand and take Noah from him.

"I hope your dad is okay," Sebastian says, standing as well, jaw tight, his expression still holding a look of accusation. "He's a good guy. He didn't deserve this."

He turns, slaps Kane's shoulder, then walks back to the group of men who keep casting guarded glances at me.

"He thinks this is my fault," I say, fighting the emotion that keeps threatening to spill over.

Kane's nostrils flare and he glares at Sebastian, who's still watching us. "Did he say that?"

"No. But he warned me not to hurt you."

"Don't worry about him. He's just pissed that I didn't tell him about us."

I place Noah over my shoulder and rub his back. "They all know now."

"Yeah." A small smile tugs at Kane's lips, and he places his large palm over mine on Noah's back, a look of pride in his eyes. "They do."

God, this man. He undoes me. I spent so many years fighting him. Blaming him. And yet, the way he looks at me, like I'm the most precious thing in the world, makes my insides melt. Brick by brick, he's torn down the fortress I'd built to protect my heart. The problem is, it's left me vulnerable.

I lean into him, and he wraps his arms around me, creating a cocoon for Noah and I.

"Have I told you how much I love you, Jacobs?" he whispers in my ear.

"I could handle hearing it again," I mumble against his chest.

"You're my world, Brynne." He cups my jaw, brushing his lips across mine. It's gentle and sweet, and I swear I hear every woman in the room sigh at the same time. "You and Noah. And whatever happens, we'll get through it together."

I believe him. More than that, I trust him.

I place my hand on his cheek and prepare myself to say the words I've been holding back. "I love-"

"Miss Jacobs?" A nurse in scrubs stands at the door holding a chart.

A nervous tension vibrates through the room which grows eerily quiet, except for the shuffling of clothes as people stand.

"That's me." I pull out of Kane's embrace and take a step towards her, shifting Noah in my arms. My whole body trembles as I wait for what she has to say.

"The surgery went well."

Relieved sighs and murmurs fill the room.

"Your father is in recovery right now. You can see him if you'd like."

I'm shaking.

"He's all right?" I ask, needing the confirmation.

"He's stable."

"Can I go with her?" Kane asks, placing his large hand on my lower back.

Strength.

Warmth.

Love.

I feel it all in his touch.

"Are you family?" The nurse asks, glancing down at her chart.

Kane starts to say no, but I interrupt him. "Yes. He's his son-in-law."

It's a small lie, but I hear the muffled whispers around the room. Kane gives me a sidelong glance, one that I don't meet.

The nurse gives us a skeptical look before nodding, and looking pointedly at Noah. "All right. But only the two of you."

"I'll take him," Sophie says as she approaches, lifting Noah from my arms before I have the chance to protest.

Kane takes my hand and we follow the nurse down a series of halls. I try not to glance into the open doors. The place smells like death mixed with antiseptic and bleach. There are sounds of constant chaotic beeping mixed with my own heartbeat that thumps wildly in my ears.

"He's in here," the woman says, nodding to a room with no door. "He should be waking up soon."

I take a step into the room, and my knees give out slightly when I see my father's hulking form spread out on the small bed, tubes and machines everywhere.

Kane is there holding my elbow, and I lean into him, using his body to keep me upright.

Time is something I've always thought I had a lot of. It plays tricks on us. Sometimes slowing down, making us think that we have eternity. Sometimes speeding up, making us wonder where we wasted all those precious minutes.

And then there are moments when time freezes altogether. Moments of clarity, moments that change us. That make us realize how short this life really is. How wrong we were to waste even a second in resentment and blame.

I suck in a shaky breath. "He looks…"

"I know." Kane kisses the top of my head. "But you heard what the nurse said. He's stable. He's going to be fine. Sit with him, Brynne."

"I don't know. Maybe he wouldn't want me here."

"He wants you here." Kane cups my chin, forcing me to look at him. "There's no one else in this world he'd rather have at his side when he wakes up than you."

The way he says it, I almost believe him. Maybe I want to believe him.

"Okay." I chew on my bottom lip and sit down beside the bed, hesitating before reaching through the metal bars to take my father's hand.

His lids flutter slightly, but they only partially open, and only for a brief moment before closing again. He makes a small, strangled sound, and the machines beep irregularly.

"Hi, Daddy."

"B-" he murmurs incoherently. "Bry-"

"You're going to be all right." I squeeze his hand, and his fingers attempt to squeeze mine back, but there's no strength in them. He opens his mouth to say something, but I shake my head. "Just rest. We can talk when you're better."

He closes his eyes, but before he drifts back to sleep, he mutters three words I haven't heard from him in a very long time. "I...love...you."

CHAPTER 28

ane

"I HATE LEAVING YOU," I murmur into Brynne's hair, holding her against my chest.

"You're only gone for a few days. We'll be okay." Her hands rest on my waist, and despite how exhausted I know she is, she smiles up at me, eyes bright with something I haven't seen in a long time – *hope*.

It's been three days since Coach had his heart attack. Three long, tiring days that Brynne refused to leave the hospital. She's home now, but I know she won't be for long.

I know she's struggling with the guilt of almost losing him when they'd been at odds with each other. And I swear she's trying to make up for all those years by being there for him now. But I'm worried she's going to burn out.

I tangle my fingers in her hair and tug gently to make her look up at me. "If you need anything-"

"I'll be fine. I was going to take Noah to the hospital today. It's time he finally meets his grandfather."

I sigh. "Are you sure you don't want to wait until I can be there with you?"

"No. There are things I need to say…" More guilt flutters across her beautiful face.

"Okay." I cup her chin, then kiss her hard, wishing I could pour all my strength into her.

"I just hate that you have to deal with all this alone."

She gives a small shrug. "At least I don't have to worry about the art exhibit anymore."

I pull back slightly and frown. "Your show. With everything that's been going on, I forgot about it."

"Apparently, so did I. I lost my spot because I didn't get my pieces to the gallery on time."

"Shit. I'm sorry. I know how much it meant to you."

She shrugs, but I can see the disappointment in her eyes. "There'll be others."

I pull her against my chest and kiss the top of her head, feeling somewhat responsible. "Is there anything I can do?"

"Actually." She chews on her bottom lip for a second before continuing. "I wanted Felix to come over and take a look at my new pieces."

"Felix?" My lips tug down as I remember the look of the guy, or more specifically, the way he looked at Brynne.

"I know it's awkward. You can say no-"

"No. It's fine. This is your home." I drag my thumb along her jaw. "You don't have to ask me to have people over."

"Good." She smiles. "Because I asked Kiley to come stay with me while you're out of town."

I grunt.

She chuckles, then stands on her tiptoes to kiss me. "I guess a grunt is better than a no."

CHAPTER 29

rynne

My father is sitting up, flirting with the nurse who's taking his blood pressure when I walk into his room. He looks better. There's a bit of color in his cheeks. But not as much as the pretty young thing who seems to be enjoying his attention.

Sunlight floods through the large windows, and countless bouquets and balloons make it look more like a floral shop than a hospital room, which makes me chuckle, because one thing my father hates is flowers and shows of affection.

"Hi." I push the stroller into the room.

"Brynne." The light humor that was in his eyes a second ago disappears.

"Is this a bad time?"

"I'm just finishing up here," the nurse says, patting my father's arm.

I wait in silence until she leaves, watching the door slowly shut behind her.

Noah stirs in his stroller, letting out a small cry, breaking our silence.

I unbuckle him, and lift him up to my shoulder.

My father tries to shift on his bed, but he winces and falls back into his semi-upright position.

"Don't strain yourself," I say.

"I want to see my grandson," he says in his typical clipped manner. "Bring him here."

I sigh, a small smile tugging at my lips, because some things will never change. I remove the distance between us, shifting Noah so that my dad can see him.

Something flickers in my father's eyes. A touch of emotion that I rarely see.

He raises his arms to take Noah from me.

"I don't think that's a good idea-"

"And I didn't ask for your advice. Now, let me hold him."

I exhale heavily and place Noah in his arms, who looks up at him and starts to babble happily.

"He's a good-looking boy," he says.

I nod, swallowing past the lump in my throat.

Noah's little fist wraps around one of my dad's fingers and he continues to gurgle and coo.

"Thank you for bringing him." He doesn't look up at me when he says it, just continues to watch Noah, affection filling his dark eyes, and for a second I swear I see tears there.

My breath is shaky when I suck it in. "I know I should have told you sooner."

"We've both done things...Made mistakes."

"Yeah." I lick my lips, shifting uneasily beside the bed.

He looks up at me, holding my gaze. "I know why you blame me for Sam."

"Dad. I-"

"Let me finish. I need to say this." His brows draw down, his expression serious. "I wasn't there for either of you when you were young. Not the way I should have been. I can give you excuses, but I won't."

I sit down on the chair beside the bed. "I know it must have been hard after Mom died."

"I'll admit I didn't know what I was doing. And I was…" He motions for me to take Noah, who's starting to squirm in his arms.

I pick him up, then place him back in his stroller, turning it so that my dad can still see him.

We sit in silence for a few long moments.

"I was gutted after your mother died." He holds my gaze with the same hard eyes that I'd never understood. My eyes. Soft, brown, rimmed with flecks of gold. But it's the soul behind them that I recognize now. Filled with pain. Loss. Sorrow.

Maybe Kane is right, and I'm not so different from him as I thought.

"You never talked about her."

"I should have." He rests his head back on the pillow, his eyes closing for a brief moment. When he opens them again, they're misted over. "You look like her. Except your eyes. You always had my eyes."

"And your stubbornness," I add.

He chuckles. "Yes. And that." His smile quickly fades, and he says, "Maybe if your mother had a bit of your spirit…"

I frown at him. "You always said I was like her."

He shakes his head. "I was worried you were."

"I don't understand. You loved her."

His lips tug down and he wipes his palm across his face. "More than anything in the world. I would have done anything for her. Would have given up my career if she'd asked. Done anything to still have her here with me. I blame myself every day..."

"She was in a car accident. It was no one's fault."

He shakes his head. "It wasn't an accident."

"But you said-"

"I tried to protect you and Sam. It was hard enough losing your mother. You didn't need to know that she..." He glances away, grimacing.

"That she what?" Goosebumps prickle my arms.

He lets out a long, quivering breath. "She was passionate. So full of life. Then there were times..." His eyes close briefly, the lines in his face becoming more pronounced. "She was pulled into a darkness. A place I couldn't reach her. It got worse after she had you and Sam. The sadness. It ate away at her. Until..."

"She killed herself?" Ice spreads across my skin. All I can think about is Sam.

He gives one small nod.

I sit back in the chair, pressure building in my chest.

"She was bipolar. I didn't know when we got married. Not that it would have changed anything. I loved her. Loved her highs. The way she thought she could conquer the world. But her lows...they were brutal. And each time she hit rock bottom, I knew I was only one step closer to losing her for good."

Bipolar. I don't know much about the disorder, other than what I read in my first-year psychology textbook. It's one of those mental health issues that still has a stigma around it.

"I know I was hard on you, Brynne. I tried to make you strong." He reaches out for me to take his hand, but I sit there, numb, trying to process everything he's saying. He gives a small, sad smile. "But you always were tougher than I gave you credit for." He sighs, pulling his hand back. "It was Sam that I should have been worried about. But by the time I realized what was going on with him, it was too late."

My head is spinning as I try to make sense of what he's saying. "You're saying Sam was...No. I would have known."

"He was diagnosed a year before..." My father swallows hard. "But I knew before then."

"Why didn't you tell me?"

"He didn't want me to. He loved you so much, Brynne. He didn't want you thinking bad of him."

"I wouldn't have. Maybe I could have helped."

"It's what he wanted. I don't even know if I should have told you now. But I think there've been too many secrets between us."

"Does Kane know?"

He nods, making my stomach sink. "He was the one who came to me. Told me there was something going on with Sam. I didn't want to believe it at first. But the drugs. The wild, reckless behavior. They were just a symptom of the disorder. If I would have been paying closer attention, I might have been able to help him."

My stomach twists.

"I failed you both. And I'm sorry."

I don't correct him. Maybe I should. But I don't.

"The ironic part was I lost you both because I was afraid to lose you." There's desperation in his words, and a resignation that stirs a small ounce of sympathy for the man.

I reach across and take his hand. "You haven't lost me. I'm still here."

His fingers squeeze mine. "I want to be part of your life. Part of Noah's life. If you'll let me. Maybe I'll be a better grandfather than father."

"There's still time to be my dad. Unless, of course, you have plans to trade Kane," I joke, making him smile.

He chuckles. "Trust me, the thought went through my

head. But I don't want him taking you and my grandson to another city. That's assuming you two are together."

I shake my head at his lack of subtlety. "We are."

"Good."

I raise an eyebrow. "I didn't think you'd have a problem with him. He's already a son to you."

"He is." His expression goes serious. "But that's not why I approve. He cares about you. Always has. I've watched that boy with you. I'm just surprised it took him this long to make a move."

"You might be surprised, but it was actually me who made the first move."

I laugh and he shakes his head. "No, darling. That doesn't surprise me at all."

CHAPTER 30

ane

"Nothing's changed in the last ten minutes," Blake says gruffly, when I check my phone for a message from Brynne.

I grunt and put it in my bag before starting to undress.

It's the first game we've played without Coach on the bench, and the locker room is filled with tension. There's a strain between the men and I know it's because of me. Blake has been a moody son-of-a-bitch since we got on the flight to come here. Sebastian won't speak to me. And the other guys keep tiptoeing around me like I've got the fucking plague.

No one speaks. Only the odd muffled curse. There's just this bloody silence filled with accusation and suspicion.

Until Tyler Slade walks into the room. Black hair slicked back, dark eyes shiny with mischief, he's got a smirk plastered on his ugly, pot-marked face. The kid is like adding gasoline to an already simmering fire, and I know there's going to be trouble the second he opens his mouth.

"Holy shit, man," Tyler says, punching my shoulder and laughing raucously. "Rumor has it you knocked up Coach's daughter. No wonder the man had a heart attack."

"Fuck off, Slade." I give him a warning glance, but he doesn't seem to notice, or he doesn't care.

"I don't blame you. The chick is hot."

"Shut it, asshole," Sebastian grumbles beside me.

"Jesus, you guys are too fucking serious. I'm just saying, if I'd had the chance, I'd totally have done her."

I place my palm on Sebastian's chest when he starts to stand.

Tyler throws his jacket down on the bench and continues like he's not aware of the friction he's causing. "I mean, since we're all into family sharing, mind if I have a go at that sister of yours when Starowics is done with her?"

He doesn't see the punch coming. Neither do I. One second Blake is sitting on the bench, the next he's on top of the kid, his fist smashing into Slade's jaw.

Sebastian and I jump on him, pulling him off, but he fights us.

"Calm down." I slam him up against the wall, my forearm against his throat.

"Did you hear what he said?" Blake struggles against me. He's big, but I'm bigger. And I'm able to hold him back.

Tyler touches his bloody lip, then spits. "It was a fucking joke. Jesus, man."

I have no clue how the kid even knows about Kiley, but there's something in the way his lips curve up slightly, a hidden knowledge in his eyes, that makes me uneasy.

"You're a douche, you know that, Slade?" Sebastian says, standing in Tyler's way so he has to go around the other side of the benches.

"How does he even know about her?" I hiss, releasing Blake.

"He lives in the building." He glares at Tyler, who's still smirking at him, albeit on the far side of the room. "He saw us together."

No. It's more than that. The kid isn't smart enough to put two plus two together, let alone figure out that Kiley's my sister.

The guys are watching us, and more than a few brows are raised.

I turn on them, and growl out, "None of this shit is any of your business-"

"When it messes with the team, it is our business," Sebastian says, leaning against the wall, arms crossed. "You've been a real asshat this past year. And now Blake has a pickle up his ass about something, which obviously has something to do with you."

"We can talk about this later."

"No. Fuck this shit. Since when do we hide things from each other? And why the hell does the kid think you're screwing Kane's sister?" He scowls at Blake, then at me.

"Kiley's been staying with me," Blake mutters. "I'm just helping her out."

"Helping her with your tongue down her throat," Tyler says, a cocky ass grin spreading across his face.

"Fuck off, Slade," the three of us say in unison.

"As entertaining as this is," Matt says, tossing a towel at us. "We've got a game to get ready for. Think you can get along for a few hours?"

"Yeah," Sebastian grumbles, sitting down on the bench and pulling out his skates. Blake nods as well.

"You're acting like pussies," Austin Branson says across from us, dragging his hand through his blonde hair, then placing his helmet on. The kid is just as vulgar as Tyler, but when he speaks there isn't the same animosity in his words. Just the boorish truth. "And why, because of a pair of tits? Hope they're worth it. Because if you assholes don't get your head out of your asses, you've already lost the game for us."

 rynne

"ARE you sure you don't mind taking him?" I ask as I hand Noah over to Kiley.

She gives me one of her rare smiles. The bruises have started to fade, and she's put on a few pounds since she's been staying with Blake, but there's a sadness in her eyes that never seems to go away.

"I'm happy to help."

"Thank you." Felix is coming over soon to look at my new pieces, and after that I could really use a nap myself. I haven't slept much this past week, and even less since Kane has been gone.

"I'll take him back to Blake's apartment for his afternoon nap." She puts him in his stroller, then takes the diaper bag from me. "That way you don't have to rush."

"You're a saint. You know that?"

She blushes and looks away.

"I'll order Chinese tonight, and we can watch the game together."

"Sound good."

When she's gone, I tidy up quickly, but I don't have much time before I get the call from the front desk letting me know Felix is here.

I'm nervous. Other than Kane, I haven't shown anyone the new pieces I've been working on.

They're different. A lot different than anything I've ever painted. But I think they're good.

Of course, Kane thinks they're brilliant. But I swear I could paint a giant red dot on a blank canvas and he'd think the same thing.

"You look good," Felix says when I answer the door, his dark eyes roaming down my body in a way that makes the hairs on the back of my neck stand on end.

I don't know if he's always looked at me that way or if I just never noticed it before, but it makes me uncomfortable. And for a second, I hesitate before widening the door and letting him in.

"Nice place." He walks in, his posture tense, nostrils flaring as he looks around. "It always shocks me how much money these athletes make. I mean, seriously, half of them have the emotional and intellectual IQ of a five-year-old, and they're making millions. Blows my mind."

I open my mouth to argue, but I realize that he's just repeating the same monologue I used to say, even though I know the truth. The men who've made it as far as Kane have worked their asses off to get where they are.

"Come on. I'll show you what I've been working on."

Felix reaches for my hand, his attention back on me. "That...*boyfriend* of yours, he's out of town, right?"

"He'll be back tomorrow." Unease settles in my stomach. I

pull away from his grip, but he hesitates before releasing my hand.

"Then we have all night."

"Excuse me?" I take a step back, putting distance between us.

"I'm kidding, Brynne." He chuckles, but it doesn't hold any humor.

"Right." I chew on my bottom lip.

"But you could offer me a glass of wine."

It's something I would have done without hesitation in the past. I can't count the number of bottles we finished together over the years.

Maybe it's me who's being weird and awkward.

This is Felix.

One of my best friends.

The man who was there for me when no one else was.

"Um."

"Come on, Brynne." He gives me a lighthearted smile. "We're celebrating."

"Celebrating?"

"I wasn't going to say anything yet, but I spoke with Gisselle Peppers, and I may have gotten you a spot in her gallery next month."

"You're kidding?"

"She just wants to see one of your pieces."

"Oh my God," I squeal, which is something I never do, and throw my arms around his neck. "Thank you."

"You know I'd do anything for you." He holds me a little tighter, and when I try to pull away, he hesitates.

"Felix," I warn.

"Sorry. Hard habit to break." He lets me go. "Now let's get that glass of wine."

Forgetting my initial unease, I lead him into the kitchen and pull out a bottle of Chardonnay from the wine cooler.

"Where's Noah?" he asks, taking the glass I hand him.

"A friend's watching him."

"Too bad. I was hoping to see him. I bet he's getting big."

"He is." Guilt creeps into my chest. I've been a terrible friend lately. Especially after everything he's done for me. "I'm sorry I haven't called. Things have been hectic here."

"I heard about your father."

Everyone has. It had been all over the news, which only pissed the man off more than he already was. Because one thing Steve Jacobs hates is being seen as weak.

I take a sip of my wine, and I let him talk, listening to him go on about his latest projects. We quickly fall back into our old easy dialogue.

Almost an hour goes by, and I'm shocked when I realize we've finished off the bottle of wine.

He lifts the empty bottle and raises a brow. "Another one?"

"No. I better not." I'm already feeling a little wobbly and lightheaded.

"Always a lightweight." He chuckles. "Why don't you show me those new paintings?"

He's close, closer than he needs to be when he follows me down the hall toward the room where my work is set up.

"So, this is what you left me for." He goes to the windows and stares out at the city below. "Can't say I blame you."

I frown, because I can't tell if he's joking or being serious. "Felix."

He turns, his hands shoved in his pockets, expression casual. But there's something in his eyes that I can't read. Something dark. And a small shiver of fear races down my spine.

"Here..." I swallow past the lump that's formed in my throat and move towards the large canvas that I finished working on yesterday. "What do you think of this one? Maybe you could show it to-"

His arms wrap around me, and he pulls my back against his chest.

For a heartbeat, I freeze.

Shit.

I turn, trying to move away, but when I do he traps me. "Felix, don't-"

His breath is heavy in my ear. "These pieces. They're fluff. You're better than this. Better than *him.*"

"Stop." I get loose from his grip, but only for a moment, before he grabs my wrists, then tugs me back towards him.

"You need me, Brynne." He pushes me so that my back is against the wall, and causing the canvases that were stacked against it to topple over.

"Let me go."

Fear sucks my breath away, choking me.

"This isn't you. You told me that you wanted away from this life. These people. You were happy when it was just the two of us." He has my hands pinned at my sides. He's not as big as Kane, but he's a hell of a lot stronger than I am.

I twist my wrists, and I'm able to get one free. Raking my fingernails across his cheek, I scream, "Get off of me!"

I see shock register in his eyes, but it's quickly replaced by anger.

"Bitch." He backhands me hard, and I taste blood on my lip as I crumple to the ground.

"Hey, asshole." A woman's voice makes us both jerk our attention to the door.

Kiley stands there, and it takes me a moment to register what she has pointed at him.

A gun.

Shit.

"Jesus," Felix breathes out, placing his hands up in the air, and taking a step backwards, putting a foot through one of my paintings. "What the hell?"

"What do you want me to do with him?" Kiley asks, her blue eyes cold and trained on Felix.

Felix looks at me, and the expression of terror on his face would almost be comical if I wasn't worried that Kiley might actually put a bullet in his chest.

"Get out of here," I say to him, using the wall to help me stand.

He takes a step towards me. "Brynne, I didn't mean-"

The click of the hammer being pulled back has us both twisting our heads towards Kiley, and my mouth drops open in shock.

"Just go. Before this gets worse," I say, flinching when he takes a step towards me.

"You want me to call the cops?" Kiley asks, but I can hear the hesitation in her voice, and I doubt she has the proper papers to be using the weapon in her hands.

"No." I stare at Felix. "He'll leave. And he'll never come back. Right?"

"Yeah. I'll go," he grits out. "But good luck ever finding anywhere to show this shit you call art. You're nothing without me. You'll always be nothing. Just a spoiled little rich girl living off other people's money."

I shrug, trying to hide the way my fingers tremble. "Maybe. But if you're not out of here in thirty seconds, you'll be nothing, too. Just an obituary in the back of the newspaper."

It's an empty threat. But he doesn't need to know it.

His nostrils flare and his lips twist in a scowl before he storms out of the room. Kiley follows him, and I sink to the floor, my legs giving out on me, and let the tears I'd been holding back stream down my cheeks.

A few seconds later, Kiley is beside me, the gun gone. A

look of protectiveness straining her pretty features. A look that reminds me of Kane.

"You okay?"

"Where's Noah?"

"Asleep in his stroller. He's fine. I just came back to get another bottle." She winces, and looks down sheepishly. "I had a little accident with the first one."

I huff out an unsteady breath. "Lucky for me."

I don't know what Felix would have done if she hadn't stopped him. I shiver, not wanting to think about what could have happened.

She chews on her bottom lip. "You won't tell Kane about the gun, will you? It's not loaded, I swear."

"It wasn't loaded?" I stare at her in bewilderment. It takes some kind of balls to point an unloaded weapon at someone.

She shakes her head and I start to laugh. I don't even know why, but I can't stop.

"My God. You're…"

"Crazy? Yeah, I know." She laughs with me.

"I was going to say fearless."

Her expression sobers. "Fear is why I have the gun."

I squeeze her hand. "You don't have anything to worry about anymore."

"Just protecting you from stalkers." She raises an eyebrow.

"Yeah." I touch my lip. It's starting to throb, and when I pull my fingers away, there's blood on them.

"Kane is going to freak when he sees that." She stands, then holds out her hand to help me up.

I wince, thinking about Kane's reaction when I tell him.

He'd warned me about Felix, but I hadn't really seen how strong his obsession was. Kane will want to know what happened, and as much as I want to protect Kiley, I have to tell him about the gun.

"I can't keep this a secret from him. You know that?"

She swallows hard. "I know."

"I doubt he'll condone you carrying a gun. Even an unloaded one. You protected me."

Her expression is still clouded over with apprehension.

I pull her into my arms and hug her hard. She resists it at first, but eventually her body relaxes and she hugs me back.

I'm still shaking, and I double and triple-check that the apartment door is locked before calling down to the front desk to let them know not to allow Felix into the building again.

I want to ask Kiley about the gun. There's so much about the girl that I don't know. But one thing I do know is she's a lot more like Kane than he thinks.

CHAPTER 32

ane

DESPITE GETTING THE WIN, the tension between the team is still tangible. I've never heard more muttering from the men since we lost in the semifinals two years ago.

Blake has done his best to avoid me. And Sebastian is still acting like I killed his fucking puppy.

After our flight takes off, I move to the empty seat beside Sebastian. "You not talking to me now?"

He gives me a sideways glance. "You still keeping shit from me?"

"You know everything."

He grunts. "I can't believe you have a kid and didn't tell me about it."

"Things were messy. I was doing my best just to keep my head above water."

"Could've helped you."

"Yeah." I admit. He's right. "Forgive me?"

He grunts. "You owe me."

"Fine." I smile. "You can have that bottle of Dalmore you've been begging me for."

"I'll take it. But I'm talking big-time owe me." He's smirking now. "Like best man at your wedding owe me."

Exhaling, I rub my palms on my jeans and grimace. "Wish I could promise you that."

"You better not tell me you're letting Starowics take my spot."

"No. It's not that."

"You are going to marry her? Christ, you've been half in love with her-" He stops and winces. "Shit. You asked her?"

"Yeah."

He gives me a look of pity. "Take it she said no."

"Smart guy." I let the sarcasm drip from my words.

"So, what? You just going to keep playing house?"

"For now."

Silence stretches between us.

"Well, then I expect to at least be the kid's godfather."

I chuckle. "Deal."

"I get the kid and Blake gets your sister. Sounds fair." He smirks at me.

"Fuck off."

"You should talk to him. He's always been a moody bastard. But I've never seen him like this."

"I know." I've been worried about him, too. But if what Tyler said is true, then I have a whole other reason to be concerned.

I get up and move down the aisle, giving Matt, who's sitting beside Blake, a look that makes him move.

"About time you two kiss and make up," Matt says with a smirk, before moving down the aisle.

Blake glances over at me when I sit down beside him, then looks back out the window.

"Well?" I ask, watching him.

"Well, what?" His voice is clipped with irritation.

"You know what."

"I didn't kiss her, if that's what you're asking. The little prick thought he saw something. But I haven't touched her. Wouldn't. She's a fucking kid. And she's your sister."

I believe him. But there's more that he's not telling me.

"You care about her."

He exhales heavily and closes his eyes. "I'm doing her, and *you*, a favor. Don't make it anything more than it is."

"So, your pissy mood has nothing to do with her?"

He glares at me.

"Good. Then you'll be happy to know that an apartment opened up in the building. I'll move her into it next week."

His brows draw down. "You think she's okay living on her own?"

"She's almost twenty years old. She doesn't need a babysitter."

He doesn't look convinced.

"I'll take care of her." I rub the back of my neck. "You were right. She's family. And Brynne seems to really like her."

"You would, too, if you took the time to talk to her."

"Maybe. But she's not your responsibility anymore."

He grunts and looks back out the window.

"We good?"

"Yeah," he mumbles, despite the lack of change in his mood. "We're good."

I return to my seat, catching Sebastian's gaze when I walk back.

He gives me a smirk and says half-joking, "I better be your best man over that moody bastard."

"If you can convince the woman I'm worth wasting the rest of her life on, then it's all yours."

rynne

IT's late and I'm in bed reading when I hear the shuffling of feet down the hall. Even though I know it's Kane, I can't help the small shiver of anxiety that races through me. Every creak and rattle has made me jump after what happened with Felix. Tonight's been the worst since I sent Kiley back to Blake's apartment, so I could be alone with Kane when he got home.

The bedroom door opens, and I let out a small relieved breath when I see him.

"You better not be wearing anything under that t-shirt." He chuckles, pulling off his shirt as he makes his way to the bed.

I laugh and place my book on the nightstand.

"You have no idea how much I missed you." He crawls across the bed, dimples shadowing his cheeks, blue eyes flashing in the dim light.

God, he's sexy.

He kisses me, and I do my best not to wince, but he must feel it, because he pulls back, his gaze questioning.

There's a small scab on my lip from where Felix hit me. I was able to cover the bruise with make-up, but I know the second he sees it.

He sits up, pulling me with him, his fingers roaming over my face. "What the hell happened?"

I sigh, placing my palms on his chest. "You promise not to get upset?"

"I'm already upset." I can see the fire in his eyes.

I tell him what happened. Every detail. Not wanting to keep anything from him anymore.

"He hit you?" Kane starts to get out of bed, but I grab his hand.

"I hit him first if that makes you feel any better," I say lightly, but he doesn't smile.

"And why the hell does Kiley have a gun?"

"It wasn't loaded."

He drags his fingers through his hair, making it stand on end. "I knew I shouldn't have left you. Not with her."

"This wasn't Kiley's fault. I don't know what would have happened if she hadn't been here."

His jaw muscle pulses rapidly. "You should have called the police."

"He won't be back." I don't tell him that I was worried about Kiley getting in trouble.

"You don't know that. We should at least put a restraining order on him."

"If he tries contacting me again, I'll think about it. But I really think Kiley scared him."

Kane sighs, then leans back against the headboard and closes his eyes. "God, I hate leaving you."

"And I hate you leaving." I move, slinking across his body

211

so that I'm straddling him, and running my fingers down his chest.

"You missed me?" He lifts a brow.

"Maybe a little." A smile tugs at my lips as I lean over and kiss his chest, dipping my fingers into the waist of his pants, hoping to divert his attention. He lifts his hips as I shift his pants down, allowing his already hard cock to spring free.

"I think you missed me more than a little." His hands slink under the oversized t-shirt I'm wearing. His palms run over my thighs, then grip my hips.

I shrug, like his touch doesn't send a thousand little sparks of ecstasy shooting through my body. But when his hand moves further up, cupping my breasts, his thumbs flicking my already hard nipples, I can't help the small cry that escapes my lips.

"Admit that you missed me." His hot mouth takes my nipple and I whimper. He gives a small, almost painful suck, then says, "Admit it, or I'm going to have to remind you how much you really missed me."

"Maybe I need to remind *you*." I wrap my arms around his neck, lifting up and positioning his cock at my entrance.

"Jesus, Brynne."

I slide down on his rock-hard warmth, groaning as I take every delectable inch of him. His fingers grip my hips and he lets out a moan of his own.

"My God. What you do to me."

I raise my arms when he pulls my t-shirt up and over my head, then tosses it across the room.

"Too much clothing," he murmurs, his mouth finding my nipple again, his large arms wrapping around my back, one hand gripping my ass as I start to move on top of him.

We start slow, but the days apart have felt like torture, and my own desperate need for him escalates, returned by his own demanding rhythm. His hands and mouth are everywhere. Touching. Licking. Kissing.

Heart.

Mind.

Soul.

And I realize that this is what it means to belong to someone. To be fully enraptured.

"Mine," he growls against my neck as he flips me over on my back, only unlocking our bodies for a brief second before he fills me again, deeper than before.

I whimper against his kiss as our bodies move in perfect harmony. His mouth devours mine, his tongue sweeping past my lips, while his fingers palm my breast, squeezing my nipple, and causing a bolt of ecstasy to go straight to my clit.

"Kane," I whimper, the pleasure coursing through me almost too much to bear.

His thrusts become harder, more desperate, and I know he's close. "Come with me, sweetheart."

I do.

Waves of pleasure rip through me until my entire body is weak and shaking, my legs boneless.

Kane lets out a groan, plunging into me one last time before his body jerks and he comes in hot, hard spurts inside of me.

I whimper as I come again from the pulsing heat.

His forehead drops to mine, and he breathes out roughly. "God, I love you."

I cup his precious face in my hands and hold his gaze, his cock still buried inside of me, and whisper the words I'd been too afraid to say until now. "I love you, too."

CHAPTER 34

Three Months Later

rynne

A SHIVER of excitement races down my spine as I walk into the large room where my paintings hang on display.

It's my first exhibit, and I'm nervous. Not just for the night, but what I have planned after.

I catch a glimpse of Kane standing in the far corner holding Noah. They're dressed in matching tuxedos. My heart races a little more, hoping he doesn't freak out when I display my final piece.

"You look beautiful," Kiley says nervously when she approaches, fidgeting in the elegant black gown I bought her.

"So do you." She's still so thin, but there's color to her cheeks now, and life in her eyes.

Kane set her up in her own apartment in the same

building we live in. Far enough away that we still have our space, but close enough that he can keep an eye on her. But it's Blake who watches her now.

Dressed in a gray pinstriped suit, he approaches, looking as temperamental and brooding as usual. There's something possessive in his eyes as they narrow in on Kiley.

"Hi," he says, his voice gruff, looking like he's ready to devour her.

I haven't mentioned it to Kane, because I know he'd do one of two things—deny it, or beat Blake's head in—but the attraction is there, and from the way her gaze drops to the floor and her cheeks turn a shade of scarlet, I'm pretty sure it's mutual.

"Hi," she says in return, still not meeting his gaze.

I sigh past the awkwardness between them. "Thanks for everything you did to help tonight."

Blake gives a forced smile, adjusting his tie like it's strangling him, then nods in the direction of Kane, who's now talking to my father. "He know anything?"

"I don't think so. If he does, he hasn't hinted at it."

"I think it's romantic," Kiley says, giving me one of her rare smiles.

I hope Kane thinks the same.

A server approaches, carrying a tray of champagne flutes. I take one, but when the server turns to Kiley, and asks "Champagne?" Kane nearly bites the man's head off, grabbing the glass from Kiley's hand.

"She's too young to drink," he growls, sending the man scurrying off towards the next circle of people.

Both Kiley and I stare at him in stunned silence for a brief moment, before she mutters something and hurries away, disappearing into the crowd.

"That was a little harsh." I raise my eyebrows at him.

He glares at me, but I see all I need to in that one look. His nostrils flare and he's about to say something when Austin Branson approaches, blonde hair slicked back, cocky grin on his face. "Nice party."

"It's not a party, asshole," Blake says.

"Well, it will be, won't it?" He looks slightly disappointed. "You said-"

"It will be," I say, glancing up at the giant of a man. He makes Kane look small, but he's still lanky and boyish. Two things Kane has never been. Not since I've known him.

"Will be what?" Kane comes up behind me and kisses me on the cheek, making Noah clap his hands and laugh. For some reason, he thinks it's the funniest thing in the world whenever we kiss. "And what the hell are you doing here, Branson?"

Branson smirks, and gives the lie I told him and the rest of the Annihilators to tell if Kane asked them why they came to my exhibit. "Coach invited me. And I never turn down free food and alcohol."

Austin plucks an hors d'oeuvre off a tray when a server walks by, then pops it into his mouth with a cocky smile, causing Blake to glare at him.

Kane frowns and whispers in my ear. "You want me to get rid of him?"

I chuckle softly. "He's fine."

I wanted his whole team here for what I have planned later.

My palms tingle with nerves.

"Nervous?" Kane cups my cheek, and Noah reaches out for me.

"Very." But not for the reason he thinks.

"You shouldn't be. But you should be mingling with the people who came here tonight to see your art, and not the

216

ones who came for the free food." He cocks an eyebrow at Austin, who grins.

I kiss his cheek, then Noah's. "Thank you."

"Don't worry about us. I'll keep these buffoons out of trouble."

Smiling, I start to leave, when Blake stops me. "Hey, Brynne."

"Yeah?"

"Madden's right. You shouldn't be nervous." I know his hidden meaning, and I give him a grateful smile.

"Yeah," Austin adds, now holding two champagne flutes. "Your art stuff is sick."

"Thanks. I think."

He keeps smiling, but his attention has already diverted to a pretty waitress that walks by.

I talk to a few journalists and collectors, answering their questions and trying not to stammer over my words, while conveying the message of each piece displayed. The theme is forgiveness and new beginnings. Each painting focuses on a piece of my own life.

Most people are drawn to the large piece hanging in the center of the room, but I find my father standing alone in front of one of the smaller paintings.

Our relationship, while getting better, is still strained. It's hard to let go of years of blame and bitterness, but I'm finding my forgiveness. We both are.

He's become a large part of Noah's life, and my son loves him. In a way, he has a new start with his grandson. A chance to be there for him, like he wasn't for Sam and I. It doesn't rewrite the past, but it, in a way, changes the value of our own relationship.

Forgiveness.

New beginnings.

They aren't just in the paintings. They're in this room, living, breathing, evolving. The way life should.

"This one…" My father says when I stand beside him, not taking his eyes off the painting. "This one's my favorite."

It's a simple piece. A young father and his daughter walking along the beach. The little girl looking up at the man like he's hung the moon and stars. I was that girl once. I painted it in hopes that one day I might be able to find that feeling again.

I know now, that giant of a man, was only that – a man.

"It's one of mine, too." I take his hand and I feel him tense.

He glances down at our entwined fingers and lets out a shuddering breath. "Your mother and Sam…they'd be proud of you."

I smile, hearing the words he can't say. Stubborn. That's what Kane always calls me. I see it now in my father's eyes. The way he struggles with his own emotions. I recognize the way they choke him, strangle him as he fights for control, making him seem hard and dispassionate.

"Thank you." I lean up and kiss his cheek, then turn when someone calls my name.

"Brynne." He stops me, swallowing hard and looking down at his glass, before once again meeting my gaze, and I see tears glazing his eyes. "I'm proud of you."

I suck in my own breath and blink back the stupid tears that burn behind my eyes. "I know, Dad."

He gives me a hard nod, regaining his composure.

My chest squeezes. *And I love you, too.*

Forgiveness. Sometimes, it's a slow process. Sometimes, it happens in a moment. The important thing is that it happens.

From across the room, I catch Sebastian's gaze and he gives me a thumbs-up.

A shiver of nerves races down my spine at what it signals.

"It's almost time," Kiley says, chewing on her bottom lip. "You ready?"

"I think so."

With a deep breath, I square my shoulders and focus on why I really came here tonight – *I love Kane Madden.*

CHAPTER 35

 ane

I'M SO FUCKING proud of her.

Dressed in an elegant, silver gown, holding a champagne flute, Brynne stands in the center of the room surrounded by art critics, journalists, and our friends. People who came here tonight just to see her work.

I'm not really sure why half the hockey team is here, but hell if I'm not glad they are. I love showing her off.

She lets out a small laugh, her eyes shining with pride as she talks about the main piece in the center of the room.

A six by six canvas hangs on a floating wall behind her. At first glance, the painting looks like a young man with his face buried in his hands, but depending on the angle, the image changes, or at least seems to. An old man. A young boy. But what's fascinating are the emotions that seem to dance off the canvas. It's not just me. I see the way people react. Fascination. Awe. Wonder.

I have no doubt that she'll sell all of her pieces.

"Mama," Noah says in my arms, pointing a chubby finger at Brynne.

"Mama's busy." I tickle him and he lets out a hoot of laughter. "You need to be quiet."

I didn't think it was a good idea bringing him, but Brynne insisted. And I'll do anything for her. Even drag a seven-month-old to an art exhibition.

Brynne's gaze lands on me and her smile broadens, causing my heart to speed up the way it always does when she looks at me like that.

"Hey," Sebastian slaps me on the back, grinning from ear to ear like the damn Cheshire cat.

"You look like you're up to trouble," I mumble, giving him a sidelong glance.

"Is it that obvious?" He reaches out for Noah, who goes to him easily. "Mind if I take him for a few minutes? The kid's a chick magnet."

I laugh because Sebastian has never had any issues in the women department, other than that they like him a little too much. Even got himself a stalker for a while.

"Need a new wingman now that you're taken." He winks at me.

Blake comes up behind me and slaps me on the back. "You ready?"

"For what?"

He nods and I follow his gaze.

Brynne is standing on the raised platform near the back of the room. A soft spotlight shines down on her, making her gown shimmer. She's looks radiant, and her eyes sparkle with a mix of excitement and fear as her gaze finds mine.

A soft hum comes from the microphone she's holding, and it cracks briefly before she speaks into it. "Hello."

The room quickly quiets, all heads turning in her direction.

"I wanted to say a quick thank you to everyone who came here tonight." The mic cracks again and I hear her unsteady breath. "This has been a dream come true, and I'm grateful to everyone who helped make it happen."

A small round of applause goes through the room.

She tugs her bottom lip between her teeth and waits a second before continuing, "Each painting you see here tonight represents a moment in my past that made me who I am today. Some good. Some bad."

Her gaze focuses on me, and I see the small quiver of her lip.

"But I have one last piece that I want to share with you all tonight. This one is different. Instead of my past, it's my future. At least, I hope it is…"

Her shoulders rise and fall as she sucks in a deep breath, then turns slightly and pulls the cover off the mounted canvas behind her.

A gasp goes through the room.

It takes me a moment, probably longer than it should, to register the words written on the canvas behind her.

Will you marry me?

All eyes are on me, but it's only Brynne that I see.

"Well, Madden?" Her voice trembles with the slight hint of fear.

Blake slaps my back, knocking the wind back into me. "Don't be a chump. Answer the woman."

Five long strides and I'm across the room, scooping her into my arms, and crushing my lips against hers. I hear the microphone drop, the sharp static sound as it hits the floor, then the cheer from the people around us.

I press my forehead against hers.

"So, that's a yes?"

I chuckle. "I thought you'd never ask."

A smile tugs at her lips. "Then how about right now?"

"What?"

Focused on Brynne, I didn't notice the clergy woman who stepped on the platform with us.

"I don't want to wait any longer." Brynne's palms are on my cheeks. "I want to be your wife. I want to be a family."

"We're already a family." I press my lips to hers. "But being your husband would make me the happiest man alive."

I kiss her again, and another cheer goes through the room.

The clergy woman clears her throat and says lightly, "Usually, we leave that part until the end of the ceremony."

We say our vows in front of our family and friends, and all throughout I can't stop thinking how lucky I am.

"I can't believe you planned this without me knowing," I say, when we finally have a second alone.

"It was difficult. You're always so damn nosy. But Blake and Sebastian helped a lot."

"I knew they were plotting something."

She grins. "Sebastian was pretty upset that he wasn't able to give you a proper bachelor party."

"I'm sure he was." I shake my head, wrapping my arms around her waist, drawing her towards me.

"I have another surprise for you."

"You're pregnant?" A shiver of hope and excitement races through me.

She groans and slaps my chest. "God, I hope not. At least, not yet. We're busy enough as it is with Noah. I'd like a little time to just be *us*."

I nuzzle her ear. "I agree. But it wouldn't be that bad."

"No. It wouldn't be. But I just booked us a week in Bora Bora, and morning sickness would kind of put a damper on it."

"A honeymoon?" I quirk an eyebrow.

"Sophie and Matt are going to watch Noah. So it's just you and me-"

I kiss her hard. "Have I told you how much I love you?"

She chuckles against my lips. "A few times. But I wouldn't mind hearing it again."

"I love you, Mrs. Madden."

Her eyes twinkle. "I like the sound of that."

"So do I." Nothing ever sounded better.

ABOUT THE AUTHOR

Amazon bestselling author C.M. Seabrook writes hot, steamy romances with possessive bad boys, and the passionate, fiery women who love them.

Swoonworthy romances from the heart!

When she isn't reading or writing sexy stories, she's most likely spending time with her family, cooking, singing, or racing between soccer, hockey and karate practices. She's living her own happily ever after with her husband of fifteen years and their two daughters.

For more information:
www.cmseabrook.com
chantelseabrook@gmail.com

ALSO BY C.M. SEABROOK

Men with Wood Series

Second Draft

Second Shot

Fighting Blind Series (MMA Romance)

Theo

Moody

Irish Rockstar Series

Wild Irish

Tempting Irish

Standalone

Melting Steel

Made in the USA
Columbia, SC
29 August 2017